W9-CYT-278

What the critics are saying...

5 "...typical "Tawny Taylor-famous" sassy dialogues...This author definitely knows how to write erotica!" ~ *Katharina, Mon Boudoir*

„Talk about humor in an erotic romance." ~ *Sinclair Reid, Romance Reviews Today*

5 *Angels* "A great story line combined with an intriguing couple and some very steamy sex makes for a terrific read." ~ *Jennifer, Fallen Angel Reviews*

5 *Ribbons* "This story grabs you from the first line and stays with you after the last page is read." ~ *Cindy, The Romance Junkies*

"Fun, quick and erotic..." ~ *Vikky, A Romance Review*

Tawny Taylor

Tempting Fate

ELLORA'S CAVE
ROMANTICA PUBLISHING

An Ellora's Cave Romantica Publication

www.ellorascave.com

Tempting Fate

ISBN #1419950630
ALL RIGHTS RESERVED.
Tempting Fate Copyright© 2003 Tawny Taylor
Edited by: Martha Punches
Cover art by: Syneca

Electronic book Publication: January, 2004
Trade paperback Publication: June , 2005

Warning:

The following material contains graphic sexual content meant for mature readers. *Tempting Fate* has been rated *E-rotic* by a minimum of three independent reviewers.

Ellora's Cave Publishing offers three levels of Romantica™ reading entertainment: S (S-ensuous), E (E-rotic), and X (X-treme).

S-*ensuous* love scenes are explicit and leave nothing to the imagination.

E-*rotic* love scenes are explicit, leave nothing to the imagination, and are high in volume per the overall word count. In addition, some E-rated titles might contain fantasy material that some readers find objectionable, such as bondage, submission, same sex encounters, forced seductions, etc. E-rated titles are the most graphic titles we carry; it is common, for instance, for an author to use words such as "fucking", "cock", "pussy", etc., within their work of literature.

X-*treme* titles differ from E-rated titles only in plot premise and storyline execution. Unlike E-rated titles, stories designated with the letter X tend to contain controversial subject matter not for the faint of heart.

Also by Tawny Taylor:

Passion and a Pear Tree
Wet and Wilde
Lessons in Lust Major
Private Games
Ellora's Cavemen: Tales from the Temple IV
Body & Soul: Pesky Paranormals

Tempting Fate

Chapter One

Ever since Fate Doherty was old enough to know monsters didn't live under her bed and Santa was her dad in disguise, she'd believed her parents had made a huge mistake in naming her Fate. She suspected by doing so, they'd angered some ancient god and placed her at one end of a giant rope in a heavenly tug-of-war. Every time things appeared to be going her way, the gods would give the rope a mighty tug, and Fate would be left neck deep in an enormous mud pit. The only way she knew to combat the whims of fate was to stifle any impulsive streak, welcome routine and concentrate on a sure, practical attitude.

And this morning, that belief was upheld…in spades.

Everything started out normal enough. She choked down a diet bar while dressing for work and subjected her naturally-curly red hair to the abuse of a scrunchy. Then as usual, she dashed to her ugly, but mechanically sound 1989 Ford Escort with ten minutes left on the clock and made the twenty-minute drive to work in record time—thirty minutes.

But once she stepped into work at Love Lines, Detroit's second largest dating service, the normalcy of the day abruptly ended.

The minute she entered the glass and brick building, her assistant, Michael, pounced upon her like an Armani-clad jungle cat. "Fate, will you please tell Angela her life is not over?" He was the best admin assistant she'd ever had, well worth the bloated salary he was paid. But this morning, she questioned his otherwise keen sense of judgment. The office resembled an upset beehive. People who normally would have remained safely tucked away in their glass-walled offices scurried around like headless barnyard fowl.

Bewildered, Fate managed a grunt and a "Huh?" but got no further.

Her boss, Vice President of Sales and Marketing, Andrew Thomas, popped his head out of his office on the balcony above and said, "Doherty, my office. In five." He disappeared like a mole in Fate's favorite carnival game—the one where you slam feral-eyed heads with a mallet. She wondered where the next rodent would pop out.

Julie, the receptionist, yanked on her arm and said, "Good luck, Fate. If you're still around later, I'd like to ask you a favor."

"What's wrong, Julie?"

"Fate! Five's up. Need to talk, pronto!" Thomas said.

Ignoring him, she studied Julie's pain-stricken expression. "What the hell is going on?"

"I can't tell you."

"What did you want then?"

"Well, I was wondering...I know I'm only a receptionist, and...well..." She stopped, her face white. "I wanted to know if you'd take me in the marketing department."

Her question took Fate off-guard, making her even more curious about the hubbub around her. "Ah, okay. But I thought you were happy where you are. You ready for a change?"

"You could say that."

"Julie, you're an excellent employee. I'll see what I can do." She still sensed the girl's distress. "Are you sure you can't tell me more? Has something happened?"

"I wish I could, but I think Mr. Thomas should be the one to tell you."

Still standing in front of Julie's chrome throne, Fate searched the faces of each person dashing through the lobby.

Something big had happened.

She tamped down her curiosity and focused on Julie's duress. "You're *not* all right. Tell me what's the matter."

Julie made her way back to her seat behind the counter. "Don't worry about me, I'll be fine. You'd better go talk to Mr. Thomas."

"Guess so, he isn't usually..." She stopped herself. *What was up with him? He didn't bark at people like a — a boss.* "...so demanding," she finished. Tossing Julie what she hoped would be perceived as an encouraging smile, she walked across the lobby toward the stairs.

When she reached Thomas's office on the second floor, it was empty. *Missed him. Must be in a meeting.* With eyes dropped to the lobby below, she turned around. Would anyone tell her what was going on? She looked for Michael, but he wasn't at his desk.

Deciding she'd check back with Thomas later, she headed for her office. As her gaze slid from Michael's desk to the door, she noticed her office light was on, and the door was slightly ajar. Before she pushed it open, a shadow passed across the frosted glass wall. Someone was in there.

Of course, Thomas. He must have been tired of waiting.

Pushing the door open, she said, "Sorry, I was held up downstairs. An emergency…" She froze as she realized too late the occupant of her office was not Mr. Thomas.

"Hi ya, Doherty," said the visitor sitting in her chair with his loafer-clad feet propped upon her desktop as though he owned the place. He wore a smirk on a cocky face she wished she could forget, and his smoke-hued eyes danced with mirth.

She tried to ignore his familiar but stunning features, his dark curly hair, square jaw, shadowed hollows under high cheekbones, the mole on his left cheek. "Gabe, what the hell are you doing in my office?" She was tempted to pinch herself. This was a nightmare. Why would Gabe Ryan, her fiercest rival, the marketing director of Love Lines' competitor, the pathetic Date Doctor, be loitering in her office?

He slid his feet from her desk, sending a smattering of sticky-notes to the floor. Shaking his head and wagging a scolding finger, he said, "Now, really Fate, is that any way to greet a colleague?"

"How did you get past security?" She forced herself to ignore his jibe. He was obviously trying to shake her.

She couldn't stand being in the same room with him for another minute. Just looking at him made her stomach turn and her blood burn in her veins. Determined to maintain as much physical distance between them as possible, difficult since the phone sat directly in front of him, she scooped up the receiver and punched security's number. He'd be hauled out of there in no time, and she'd have peaceful chaos once again.

But, as she struck the last digit, Gabe stabbed at the phone with an index finger, cutting off the call. "I wouldn't do that if I were you." His voice held a hint of levity.

"What are you talking about?"

He yawned and stretched his arms over his head. "Security let me in. They're not going to escort me out."

"Who'd you bribe this time?"

"No one. I didn't have to resort to bribery. Since I'm such a great guy, they escorted me in. Damn near held a welcoming parade."

"What kind of idiot do you think I am? About the only one who'd welcome you, would be the devil himself."

"So, as self-proclaimed lead bitch and spokeswoman, I expect you to act on his behalf. How about we start off with some party games? I think I can find a bottle here somewhere." He waggled his eyebrows suggestively, the expression all too familiar.

The final thread of her patience snapped, and her mouth shifted into overdrive, "Okay, enough! I'm calling security whether you think I should or not. And I suggest you get your wide ass out of my chair and find another office to contaminate!"

He grinned and then he laughed loud and hard. Standing, he motioned to the chair. "Please, don't let me ruin your day. You want the chair, it's yours."

"Of course it's mine." *Why wouldn't it be?* "The whole office is mine, and I want you out. Out of my sight. Out of my life... Out of this world."

"Thanks, that's quite a compliment! I knew you had it in you all these years. Knew you couldn't be the cold bitch you pretend to be." He smiled triumphantly.

A compliment? "What?"

"I can think of better uses for all that wasted passion." He sauntered around the desk and poked her nose with his forefinger. "I think you're out of this world, too."

"I didn't mean it as a compliment, you idiot." Damn it, she hated how he twisted her words around to mean the exact opposite of what she'd intended.

"Well, you don't have to be insulting."

Why wasn't she getting through to this man? It was as if his skull was made of brick. She gave him a healthy shove toward the door. "Out."

"And where do you suggest I go?"

"To hell?"

He quirked a smile.

What was so funny about this situation? She had a ton of work to do. Love Lines' market share had dropped dramatically last quarter, and she was presenting a new marketing strategy to the head honchos this afternoon. But she couldn't get it finished with this orangutan in her office.

Why was Gabe Ryan so hell bent on seeing her fail? He'd have to be mighty immature to still be seeking revenge for that little misunderstanding they'd had in college. He'd tried every trick in the book over the past few years. "What is this? Another sorry attempt at putting Love Lines out of business by wasting my time?"

He smacked his forehead. "Damn, you figured me out. But alas, I didn't have to do anything to put Love Lines out of business. They did that all on their own."

"You're a moron. They're as alive and kicking as I am."

"Better check your facts, Fate, and your vitals while you're at it. From my estimation, your heart stopped beating six years ago, long before Love Lines went defunct. But what the hell do I know? I'm no doctor."

"Get the hell out!"

A couple of custodians hauled in a metal desk that hadn't seen the light of day in probably thirty years and dropped it in the middle of the floor. "What is that?" And then Julie's comment flew out of the air and, dive-bombing like a kamikaze, struck her from the rear. *What did Julie say? Something about if I was still here later…*

She dashed into the hall and upon reaching Thomas's office, opened the door and stepped in. The man sitting at the desk was not Thomas. She studied him, middle-aged, wearing a poorly fitting navy suit and a 1980's power tie. When he didn't speak she asked, "Where is Mr. Thomas?"

He slowly stood. "He's gone, Miss…"

"Gone? Where? And who are you?"

He swiped his hand down his polyester-sheathed leg and thrust it at her. "Curtis Duncan. Vice President of Sales and Marketing. And you are?"

She glared at his hand and then met his gaze. VP of Sales and Marketing? Thomas was gone? What the hell was going on? Had she inadvertently walked into the wrong office? The wrong world? She waited for the Twilight Zone music to play from hidden speakers. Was this some sick jerk's idea of a joke?

Still unable to grasp what was happening, she took his hand in hers and shook it. "Fate Doherty."

A tentative smile spread over his face, sending creases from the outer corners of his eyes up to his temples. From there, the lines plunged under his greenish-tinted rug.

15

"Miss Doherty, glad to meet you." He motioned toward the chair in front of his desk. "Why don't you have a seat, and I'll fill you in."

She hesitated, not sure if she wanted to know what was going on. It was all a bit too bizarre. Then, knowing she needed her job, to understand what was happening, she slumped into the chair and waited.

"Last week, your company was the victim of a hostile take-over."

Hostile takeover? By what, Martians? She cringed.

"I understand Mr. Thomas was fond of you. Hopefully we can share a comfortable working partnership as well."

She bit her tongue, holding back a sarcastic retort, and nodded. When the heat was on, her mouth ran out of control. High time she put that to a stop.

"As I was saying, my employer, The Date Doctor, purchased Love Lines last week. Despite your former C.E.O's attempt to purchase back controlling shares, we remain the owners of sixty-five percent of Love Lines. In order to cut costs, we have decided to combine operations and maintain one office. Since Love Lines' location is more suitable for our market, we chose to set up our new offices here."

"The Date Doctor?" Gabe! Oh God, he was now…working with *her*?

Nausea sent her stomach into relentless spasms. What was going to happen next? Surely they didn't need two marketing directors.

Duncan leaned back in his chair and continued, "We have made a handful of staff changes, mostly trimming excess. And speaking of excess, we didn't need two V.P.'s of Sales and Marketing." His smile faded as he cleared his throat. "Anyway, I have to decide how to structure the rest of the departments under my control, including yours." His gaze leveled at her.

Great, despite that little speech about working relationships, it was obvious he didn't like her already.

Her front teeth stung her bottom lip as she bit down. "I understand. I suppose you don't need two marketing directors either."

"Not exactly."

"What does that mean?"

"I'm still considering a number of different ways to structure the marketing department. In the meantime, I've decided to assign you and Mr. Ryan, whom I trust you've met, with an assignment."

"Yes, we've met," she muttered, trying to hide her loathing for Gabe behind a façade of indifference.

"Excellent. Then here's the assignment." He slid a binder toward her. "You might need this. It contains some standard marketing info on The Date Doctor, you'll need to familiarize yourself with it before you begin."

She ran her finger along the lumpy spine of the black binder and stared at the white print emblazoning the front. The Date Doctor. "Thank you."

"Now, I'm looking for something fresh. We need a new name and an entirely new way to market ourselves. No more phone soliciting. We have a great service, and I want to target the younger crowd. No more forty-something women living in trailer parks with five kids. Got it?"

She nodded. Another opportunity for sarcasm. She had great respect for women in all economic brackets and here she was with another male chauvinist.

But no, she wouldn't risk her job for a punch line.

"For the time being, I hope you don't mind sharing your office with Mr. Ryan. You'll be working together anyway, so I figure it would be good for you to share the office. Once the overall department structure is in place, we'll make more permanent arrangements."

The threat in his tone was unmistakable. Reading between his words was like reading a neon sign. Cost-cutting was a priority to the new brass. There would be only one marketing director.

And there was no way in hell she'd let it be Gabe Ryan!

* * * * *

Gabe made the last few adjustments to his new desk's placement, lifting a corner and pushing it toward the wall. When he'd been called this morning and was told to report to Love Lines, he'd no idea what was going on. Never in his wildest dreams would he have guessed the truth.

As it turned out, reality was better than his wildest dreams. Yesterday, he'd been the marketing director of a mediocre dating service. Not the most rewarding job he'd ever held—certainly not the kind of job he'd dreamed of as he'd slogged through four years of college and two years of grad school. He'd be in debt for the next ten years, all for a crummy job selling memberships to a dating service.

But, that was *yesterday.*

Today, a god had knocked the world on its side. And how much more pleasant this angle was—even if the blood was rushing to his head.

Six-thirty, bright and early, he'd reported to Love Lines as directed, and after learning he was sharing an office with Fate Doherty, not only his former adversary, but also a woman he'd dated and slept with briefly in college, he'd gleefully planned his next move.

Desk in place, he adjusted the white cloth vertical blinds, which had become tangled when he'd brushed against them. He peered out the window, savoring the view of the traffic-clogged road and neighboring glass and steel temples to the god of capitalism.

The memory of his earlier confrontation with Fate buzzed through his mind. Was he cruel, the way he'd toyed with her? Possibly. Did he feel guilty? A tad. But overall, he'd enjoyed their heated exchange immensely. It was better than what little interaction he'd been afforded over the last ten years.

No longer would he begrudge Monday mornings, not when he had so much to look forward to. And the new partnership between companies already stirred his creative juices. He was nearly exploding with ideas. The thought of targeting twenty-somethings, rather than the conservative thirty and forty-crowd, sent a jolt of revitalizing energy through his brain.

New name, new marketing strategy, new advertising media. Maybe television.

The only hurdle he had to overcome was also the one thing that made his new position so delightful, Fate Doherty. He needed to let her see the other side of Gabe Ryan, not a particularly settling thought.

Although he still found her absolutely stunning, with her curly copper hair, ivory skin, vivid green eyes and heart-shaped face, under the surface of that angelic veneer lay a hardened ice-queen. And the arctic slivers she shot from those emerald eyes could slice a man to pieces. She was not a woman to mess with. And he couldn't wait to do just that.

Sure, she'd grown comfortable in their adversarial relationship. Why wouldn't she? By remaining enemies, he guessed she didn't have to face any threatening emotions. But now, neither of them had a choice.

If he were a religious man, he'd be on his knees right now, thanking the gods. No doubt about it, one of them was smiling down at him. He'd been wishing for an opportunity to rekindle the explosive chemistry he and Fate had shared so long ago. At last the opportunity was his, and there was no way he would blow it.

Turning, he took in his surroundings, still not sure whether or not he was dreaming. Nope. Couldn't be a dream. In his dreams he never had such a nice office. This place was a palace compared to his cubbyhole at the former Date Doctor headquarters. The walls were pristine white, and Fate's furniture matched—definitely top dollar. Real artwork even graced the walls.

He walked over to Fate's desk, notably devoid of clutter, and scooped a framed photograph from its lacquered surface. She was accepting an award from the ex-C.E.O. of Love Lines. Tracing the outline of her face, he thought, *Fate Doherty, you have no idea what's in store for you.*

Damn, did she look sexy in the photo, even if she was wearing a conservative blue suit and overly grim expression. He couldn't wait to see her clothed in more casual attire—a pair of shorts, or sweats and one of his t-shirts. He closed his eyes and imagined the scene, sighing.

"What the hell are you doing, you psychopath?"

Her voice struck him like a bolt of lightning. His eyes flew open. "Thinking about our new partnership. What do you think about the news?"

Her eyes flashed. "I want to make one point perfectly clear. *We* have no partnership. Our companies merged, but there is no way we will be sharing anything. You understand?"

"Sure." He hadn't expected her to give in easily. Actually, the tougher she was the better. He enjoyed a challenge, especially from a woman. Once she realized he was more than a cocky, troublesome, man-boy, she'd come around. He'd have plenty of opportunity to reveal the depth of his intelligence and personality.

A grimace firmly in place, she followed his movements with narrowed eyes as he set the photograph down and returned to his junky aluminum desk. Missing a metal foot, it rocked noisily when he rested his arms on the top. No matter. He didn't need a fancy one.

He slumped into his chair and kicked his feet up on the desktop, intentionally rocking it. Even with his back turned, he could see her grimace in his mind's eye with each hollow bang. He smiled and stared at the Rembrandt print on the wall, a portrait of a man painted in dark colors. The solemn tone of the painting might have matched the former mood of Fate's office, but that was about to change.

He stood, took down the painting, and in its place hung his babe and motorcycle calendar. There. That ought to get her goat. Damn, this was fun!

Before getting to work, he took a few minutes more to rummage through his boxes, delivered by a stream of movers over the past half hour or so, and found his more charming decorations—gag gifts never meant to be on display anywhere sunlight might reach. The Whip and Chain Chiropractor coffee cup his friends had given him after he'd graduated from college, the Rodney Dangerfield talking bust his brother had thoughtfully bought him for his last birthday, and a Voodoo computer his last boss had given him after he killed three computers were the perfect compliment to his ugly desk.

Forcing his mind back to the task at hand, he slipped down deeper into his chair. Time to brainstorm, his favorite past time. "What do you think about television?"

"Huh?" was her unenthusiastic response.

He kicked his feet against the desk front, spinning his chair around. As he turned to face her, his feet slammed on the ground, stopping the momentum. "Television?"

"What about it?" She glared at him.

"I'm not trying to trap you or anything. We're on the same team now, remember?"

Pulling several files from a low cabinet next to her desk, she shook her head. In a soft tone, like a mother would use when scolding a toddler, she said, "No, we're not. There isn't room in this office for two of us. Someone will be leaving, and I'm guessing it'll be within the next week or two."

"Hmm. Hope you're wrong. Wouldn't give us much time to get reacquainted."

Clearly ignoring his comment, she continued, "The way I see it, we'll both be better off if you do your thing and I do mine. No partnerships."

"Damn! You're gonna take all the fun out of this."

"No, this is a job, and I'm taking it seriously."

"Of course you are, Fate. By the way, I've never told you, but I love your name. Your parents hippies? I never did get to meet them."

Something on her desk captured her attention, exaggerated to the point of ridiculousness. "Well, maybe if you hadn't been such an immature goon in college you might have had the chance. My parents have a warped sense of humor. I imagine you would get along with them just peachy."

He chuckled at the insult, having heard it so often it had lost its former sting. "Well, I have some great ideas about the new company. You might want to listen."

She lifted her eyes. "Okay, fire away." Her cynical expression and emotion-void voice suggested she had no interest in his ideas, but her lack of enthusiasm didn't deter him.

"I say we produce a dating program. You know, like a blind date show. We can screen the applicants and set up the dates..."

"A television program would require an enormous capital investment. Video and sound crews, producers, directors, staff to screen applicants. Where would the money come from? Last I checked it wasn't in the marketing budget." She flopped open the Date Doctor marketing binder, shuffling pages until she found the budget page. "Nope. Not there. *Sooorry!*"

Shot down. No matter. He would find a way. He rummaged around in his brain for an idea. "I know. We'll sponsor a show or provide the contestants, do the applicant screening for a show that already exists. That way, we'd get hundreds—thousands—of young singles in the door. Then we could sell them our service."

"I don't know. Your plan sounds sneaky. I don't like it."

"You have a point?"

Cutting him off again, she dropped her head and started reading.

The fun was over.

Determined to find a solution, Gabe spun his chair to face his desk and doodled on a notepad. He wasn't an advocate of team meetings or brainstorming sessions, but he was beginning to see their benefit. Fate was the perfect person to bounce ideas off, intelligent, honest, critical. If she permitted, together they could be a force to be reckoned with.

Resolved not to let her intelligence go to waste, he turned to face her. "What about a name? Any thought there?"

The paper she held slipped from her fingertips. Pushing against the desk, she scooted her chair back. Her dress, black with simple lines that traced every curve, shimmied down her body as she stood. "Mr. Ryan, I think we'd better set things straight right now."

There was no mistaking the tone of her voice. He waited with expectation. She was tough, inflexible, beautiful, and wielded a tongue as sharp as a saber. He had dreams about that tongue. A man had to be tough to stand up to her, or insane, but he was far from intimidated.

No, she was his perfect match. In every way.

She continued, "I have no choice but to accept the situation, and I suspect you don't either. I am determined to make the best of it..."

"Good, so am I."

"Would you let me finish?"

"You weren't through yet? Oh, sorry." He had to smother a laugh. Baiting Fate was his favorite hobby.

After a deep sigh and a shake of the head, she muttered, "They can't expect anyone to work like this."

"I think it's a great set-up. You're looking at the whole thing wrong. Instead of searching for a way out, you need to consider how the situation can work to your advantage. I've always done that, and I can't complain about the results. Look where I am now." To illustrate his point, he swept his hand toward his desk, presenting it like a game show hostess did a valuable prize.

She bit her quivering lip, and then the corners of her mouth lifted into a brilliant smile. "Yeah, I can see what you mean. That desk is to die for."

He stood, shook it, and kicked at the legs as though he were inspecting a used car. "Good tires, solid. What's there to complain about?"

They faced each other, and a tense silence fell between them like a curtain...electricity sizzled between them. He imagined himself pulling her to him, and planting a deep kiss on those pouty lips.

"What are you grinning about? That is the goofiest expression I have ever seen."

Her words yanked him from his musings before he'd fully enjoyed them. "Um, thinking about my game show idea. It could be a lot of fun." His cheeks reddened. Good Lord! He couldn't be blushing...*nah, must be the heat.*

"I think your idea is absolutely ridiculous. It'll never work. For one, you'll never find a show willing to let us do the screening. They look for specific things when they select contestants... Then again, maybe you should pursue it. On your own, of course. I'm going to lunch."

He shrugged. No need to sell her on his idea yet. Once he'd worked the bugs out, she'd see its genius. He was simply glad to have broken the ice a bit, eased the tension. Or—He watched her ass sway as she walked to the door. Damn, that was one round, firm ass. The heat from his face spread down his body...

What was he thinking when Fate's ass interrupted his thoughts? Shit, he had it bad.

Chapter Two
Today, of all days, am I going to be stood up?

Fate sat at the tile-topped table in the noisy restaurant, glancing at the door every few minutes. More than ever, she needed the benefit of Tracy's level-headed logic. Where was she?

The atmosphere of the restaurant was an odd melding of Tex-Mex steakhouse and English pub. Pop music blaring from speakers and diners' chattering voices did little to diminish her stress. Her heartbeat quickened with every minute that passed, and each time the waiter ran by without acknowledging her.

After another glance at her watch, she sighed and waved at him again. "When you get the chance…"

Turning, he smiled and took her order, a sandwich she could pack away or take to the office if she had to. No way she would take more than an hour. How bad would a leisurely-extended lunch look today?

As the waiter stepped away, Tracy ducked from behind him and plopped into the chair across from Fate. Studying Fate with a grimace, she asked, "What's the deal with you? On the phone you sounded like the world's come to an end."

"Thank God you're here." Fate looked at her watch. Forty-five minutes would have to be good enough. At least she didn't have to drive back to work, she'd purposefully chosen the restaurant next door to save a few precious minutes.

"Yeah, I'm here. So what's the big emergency?" Tracy wore her usual corporate black suit, and her golden hair was swept back in a French knot. Her makeup was flawless, her entire personage polished.

Fate wished she could be as collected as Tracy, especially today. "I have a big problem, and I don't mean pimple on date night big, I mean *big*, big."

The waiter stepped in before Tracy could respond and took her order. Once he was beyond earshot, Tracy rested her elbows on the table and leaned closer. "What is it?"

"Love Lines was bought out."

"Wow! When? You didn't know?"

"Nope. I stepped into chaos this morning and feel like I'm on a wild carnival ride—the Tilt-A-Whirl. I had no idea. No one did, that is, except for the brass, but obviously they didn't tell anyone."

Tracy fell back against her chair. "Wow. I know I keep saying that, but I'm at a loss. Sorry, Fate. Did you get fired?"

"Not yet. But—here's the worst part—they teamed me up with Gabe Ryan to design the new company's image and marketing strategy. We're sharing an office. It's been four hours, and I swear I'm going to hurt him by the end of the day if he doesn't shut his mouth!"

"The one you've been waging war against? Ryan from The Date Doctor?"

"The one and only. Oh, and have I ever told you we dated briefly in college? I broke it off because he was such an immature ass, and I swear he hasn't matured a day since then."

"Immature ass?"

"The man thought fine food came in paper wrappers, treated a beer keg with more reverence than me, and couldn't hold back an ejaculation for more than a minute."

Tracy's eyes glimmered as the waiter stepped in to serve their drinks and salads. Her lip quivered.

Fate could swear her friend was about to laugh. "Is something funny?"

Piercing a cherry tomato with her fork, Tracy avoided her gaze. "Funny? No. Absolutely not." She held a cupped hand over her mouth, but Fate couldn't miss the mirth in her eyes.

"Then why are you laughing?"

As Fate's last word slipped from her mouth, Tracy burst into an uncharacteristic belly laugh. "Oh, Fate, I'm so sorry. I'm not laughing at you, I'm laughing at the whole scenario."

Suddenly lacking an appetite, Fate glanced down at her tossed salad. The food held the appeal of bricks. "What's so funny about *that*? Tracy had always possessed a slightly warped sense of humor, but never had she laughed at something so serious. "I didn't laugh when your ex-boyfriend showed up on your doorstep in nothing but a leather g-string and brandishing a whip."

"That wasn't funny, it was downright scary, considering the boy had gained two hundred pounds. Sorry, Fate. Love ya like a sis, but I have to tell you, this is funny. Really funny."

"No it's not. It's just your warped sense of humor."

"Look, you've spent the last three years battling Ryan—correction, more like six years—he's been like a fly buzzing in your ear, a mischievous sprite tossing roadblocks in your way at every turn. And now he's working with you."

"Yeah, and he's still throwing roadblocks at me, but now he doesn't have to throw as hard."

"Oh, come on, Fate. He's been the sole reason you've worked so hard the past three years. Admit it, you're a competition junkie."

"Am not!"

"Look at you, you can't even deny it with credibility. Give it up. I think you still like the guy."

Whoa, was she on the wrong planet! Like *him*? Gabe Ryan? Obnoxious, immature, annoying... The vision of his mirth-filled face flashed through her mind. His eyes, which should be cold considering their steel color, were always filled with life. And his mouth was always pursed into a playful smirk, sending little creases from the corners of his eyes. And his body...shit, that body. Wide in the shoulders, narrow in the hips. Thick arms and legs, every muscle sculpted to perfection, thanks to countless hours spent in the gym or who knew what perversions.

Nope. Nothing to like there.

Even though his physical qualities wouldn't turn off any red-blooded woman, his personality would. He went out of his way to annoy people, treated women like objects, and was manipulative and sarcastic. Sure, she couldn't deny he was as full of life as his eyes, playful and easygoing, intelligent. Creative. But the bad outweighed the good by one hundred-fold. "How could I like him? He's been nothing but a thorn in my side since I met him?"

Tracy stared at her, her smile still broad as the waiter set their sandwiches before them. After he left, she challenged, "Why don't *you* tell *me*? It's all over your face, Fate. You can't lie."

"No way, you've got the wrong message. That's nausea all over my face. How can you even consider it?" She shoved her plate away. Maybe she'd eat later, or yield to the temptation to dump it on Gabe.

"Isn't there some kind of saying about love and hate being nearly the same?"

"Who knows." Fate took a drink of her diet soda, forcing the liquid past the boulder-sized lump in her throat. She didn't like the way the conversation had turned. She needed a strategy, not girl-talk. She wasn't in high school, and there was more at stake than a prom date. "Tracy, I need your help! Would you quit with the mushy stuff?"

"What's wrong? Did I hit it in the nose? Yes, I did, I'm gooood." Tracy's grin suggested she wasn't about to give up.

"No. But you have to remember what's going on here—"

"You're too wrapped up in your work, that's what's going on," Tracy interrupted, then popped a french fry into her mouth.

God, Fate hated when people interrupted her! Gabe Ryan did that too. It was annoying. "Would you let me finish? I love you to death, but you're a terrible listener."

Tracy chuckled and took a dainty bite of her sandwich. With a nod, she encouraged Fate to continue. "I'm all ears."

"I have two weeks to get the financing for my mom's house. If I don't, her bank will put it on the auction block. I can't change jobs. Not now!" From Tracy's surprised expression, Fate guessed she'd forgotten about the house. Tracy was a wonderful friend, caring and true-blue, but sometimes she was a little flighty.

After taking a sip of her diet soda, Tracy said, "Of course you can change jobs. First, didn't you get pre-approved?"

"Yup, but a pre-approval isn't written in stone, you still have to go through the formal approval process."

"But if you take a job in the same field it won't matter. At least, that's what I've heard." Tracy took another bite of her sandwich and washed it down with a gulp of soda.

"I don't think that's true for all banks." Fate watched her, wishing she could eat, but even the thought of food sent her stomach into convulsions. "I don't know. I'm not willing to take the chance. If I fail, Mom'll be out of a house. I can't believe this is happening." Her mood was sinking fast, like the Titanic into a frigid ocean.

Tracy tipped her head and regarded her with sister-like concern. "Oh, Fate. I'm sure everything will work out fine. They haven't fired you yet, right? So there's still the chance they won't." She munched on another fry, studying Fate with soft eyes and a gentle expression. Then, her mien changed, growing more determined. "What's your boss have to say about all this? Thomas, right?"

"He's gone. They fired him. I didn't get the chance to talk to him before he left."

The assuredness on Tracy's face washed away. "Oh."

Fate's hope sunk to the darkest pit—down deeper than any ocean, where there was no light and the water pressure was high enough to crush steel. As the waiter dashed by, she flagged him down and asked for a to-go box. After he nodded and stepped away, she looked at

Tracy. "I need some ideas. We have to come up with a new name, marketing concept, the whole nine yards. I've been wracking my brain all morning but haven't come up with a thing."

"Sorry, Fate. I'm an accountant not a marketing director. I couldn't come up with an original idea if my life depended on it."

"You're no help." The waiter set the white foam box next to Fate and ran off again before she could thank him. "Sheesh! I'm all for waiters who hustle, but every time I want something I practically have to wrestle him to the ground for him to stay long enough to listen." She arranged her sandwich and salad in the box and closed the lid. Then she looked at Tracy.

Tracy dropped her gaze and, biting her lip, toyed with her napkin.

"Did I say something wrong?"

"No." Tracy continued to avoid her gaze. "Although being told I'm no help isn't exactly what I wanted to hear today."

God, am I a coldhearted bitch. "Sorry, Tracy. You came at my beck and call and I insulted you. I swear I'm hopeless."

"No, you're not. You're my friend, and I wish I could help you. But I have no idea what to suggest. Are you sure they're going to fire one of you?"

She glanced down at her watch before answering. Ten minutes. "Almost positive. The new VP made it clear they don't need two heads of marketing, and since he's the former VP of the Date Doctor's sales and marketing departments, Ryan has the home-court advantage."

"What's good ole Gabe doing? Has he been real secretive?"

"No, actually, he suggested we work on the project together, but his idea is ridiculous. It'll never work."

Tracy's glum expression lightened. "Then do what he would, Badger him into quitting, trick him into leaving. That might work."

Fate grabbed her purse and fished out a ten, dropping it on the table for her share of the tab. "I'm not following you."

"Tell him two heads are better than one... Don't you love saying that? Act like you're working with him then trick him into failure. If nothing else, that might buy you some time until your mortgage is approved and you've closed on the house. Then, you could look for another job. Quit before they fire you."

"But that could take weeks. I don't know if I can work the rest of the day with him. He's such a pain in the ass."

Tracy shot her an encouraging smile. "Be a pain in the ass right back."

Fate looked at her friend, her resolve building. Tracy was right. She had to go along with Gabe's plan for a while. It might help her find a way to gain the advantage.

If only Gabe wasn't so damn maddening!

* * * * *

Gabe swept the last crumbs of his peanut butter sandwich from his desk and, forcing his attention back to his laptop, resumed reading from the animated gif-laden web page. Pictures and icons virtually bludgeoned him from all angles. This was supposed to attract him to the site?

Glancing down at his Scooby-Doo watch, a gift from his eight-year old niece, his heart leaped. Almost one-thirty. Fate would be coming back any moment now. He couldn't wait to see her. Silly, ridiculous, but nevertheless a fact.

He'd spent the last hour cramming his sandwich down his throat and wishing the hour away. It was so unlike him to go nuts over a woman. He'd quit trying to figure it out long ago. All he knew was that he couldn't get close enough to her. She was truly magnetic, fascinating, an enigma waiting to be resolved...and he was the Indiana Jones to do it.

Forcing himself to concentrate, he scanned the competition's web page for ideas. Metro Detroit had more than its share of dating services. He needed a fresh name and approach, something clever, catchy. On the web he'd found services for vegetarians, redheads, astrological, people who were looking for menages—a personal favorite—also interracial couples, inmates, various nationalities, and homosexuals.

The agencies employed wide-ranging methods, everything from biorhythm matching to videos or photos and voice recordings. How would they find a unique approach? What would be their niche?

"What's so interesting?"

Fate's voice wrenched his focus from his computer screen, and when he saw her, he silently rejoiced, his pulse trotting, his heart thumping in his ears and his face warming. She was dazzling, wearing a wide smile. Evidently she was one of those people who suffered from low blood sugar. "Hiya, Doherty. Doing some research on the web. Hoping to get some inspiration. Did you know there is a dating service that uses biorhythm to make matches? Should we check it out, see how it works?"

She remained at the doorway, lingering like she didn't know whether she was in the right office. "No, I think I'll pass. Thanks, anyway. I don't let anyone attach anything to my body, not even doctors."

"That's a damn shame," he muttered. "I could think of a few things I'd like to attach to that body..."

"What did you say?"

"I said...um, are you gonna come in? After all, this is your office."

A sexy flush spread up her neck and colored her face. She hurried to her desk and slid into the chair.

When she didn't speak, he continued, "Maybe later we can do some market research. What's on the agenda today? Have you thought about my idea?"

She rested her elbows on her desk and dropped her chin into her hands, her expression wistful—almost childlike—and utterly charming. "I did a little thinking over lunch."

"And?"

Biting her lip, she said, "I think we should work together on this project. You were right."

It took every ounce of self-control to keep from howling with glee, but he managed. And then...he wondered why she'd given in so easily. She was up to something, but he could play along for a while. Forcing a casual tone to his voice, he said, "Okay. Should we start with the target market? Or would you rather think quietly and then discuss our ideas later?"

"No, this is fine."

"Glad to see you're not still sore about this buyout thing."

Her eyes narrowed. Her mouth pulled taut. "It's been a crazy day. I have always loved my job. Had aspirations of moving up in the company. This has been a little hard to swallow, especially knowing I could end up the recipient of a pink slip."

"Yeah, it's been a bit of a shock to me too, but I'm not disappointed by the way things have turned out so far."

She laughed. "No?"

"Not at all."

They stared at each other, and he felt like he was a high school kid all over again, caught off-guard in the hallway by the head cheerleader he'd secretly pined over for months. He wondered if she could read his mind with those inquisitive green eyes.

Then, as though a shutter had snapped shut, the emotion he'd seen vanished, and her mien grew guarded again. "Let's do this." She flopped open a spiral notebook and took her pen in hand. "Let's list what is meaningful to our target market, then, hopefully, we'll find somewhere to go with it."

He enjoyed the way she took the reins. And her words possessed a trace of proposition he was certain she was not aware of. His playfulness returned. "Okay. My target—er, our target market is single, twenty-something? Right?"

"I don't think we have much of a choice in that, do we?"

There is that smile! Her whole face lit up. He hoped he would see plenty more of those after they'd both grown more comfortable with each other. He stood and walked to her desk, resting his rear end on a corner and swinging his leg. "Choice? Guess not. Now, what is meaningful to our target market? Off the top of my head, I would list television, vampire slayers, body piercing..."

Fate cringed. "Body piercing?"

He laughed. "They all have them."

"I don't get the appeal."

"I'm guessing you haven't kissed a guy with a pierced tongue?"

Her eyes widened to the size of saucers. "God, no!"

He leaned forward, until he was as close as he dared. The fresh scent of her shampoo and light citrus cologne drew him closer. "Then you don't know what you're missing." The empty hole in his tongue rubbed against the roof of his mouth. He wished he had his tongue ring in but he always took it out for work. He would give her a private showing—hopefully soon.

Still seated in her chair, she leaned away from him. "And you have?"

With forced casualty, he straightened up, inspected his fingernails and said, "Of course I have."

"I didn't know you were gay."

Her words clubbed him with dazing force, making his head spin. He lost his balance for a split second. *Whoa! Where'd that come from?* He gazed at her mischievous face, and laughed. "*Touché.*" He feigned a hairball in his throat, or otherwise massive obstruction, and dashed from the office for a drink of water. Something stronger would have been welcome, but considering he didn't drink, at least not often, he figured it would only make him lose consciousness.

Then again, maybe unconsciousness was a good thing.

He took refuge in the break room. While he was fishing amongst the lint in his trouser pocket for some change for the vending machine, Duncan greeted him with a grin. "Hey, Ryan, how are the new digs?" He clapped Gabe on the back. "I did you a huge favor, eh? You owe me, buddy."

"Sure did, Duncan. Thanks."

"You look shaken. Everything okay?"

Duncan's rug had slid a little to the left, and Gabe resisted the temptation to knock it off his head. He'd tried for years to convince Duncan the hairpiece wasn't going to make him look younger, but the middle-aged divorcé wasn't about to listen to a guy who still had a full head of hair. "Okay? Yeah, everything's okay. But I have a question for you. This morning, did you threaten to fire Fate?"

"Had to. The brass won't have two marketing directors. Don't need 'em. But I can't fire you. I gave you some time, though. Told her we would be finalizing the department's structure in the next few weeks." He studied Gabe for a minute and then added, "What's wrong with you?"

"I'll resign. Don't fire her." Avoiding meeting Duncan's gaze, he slid four quarters into the vending machine.

"What the hell are you talking about? I'm not gonna let you do that."

"You can't fire her."

"Of course I can. What are you trying to pull here? You have something to tell me?"

The soda can clunked down the chute. When it reached the bottom, Gabe gripped it and opened it with a crack. "No." He let the fizzy cold liquid wash down his throat then looked at his boss, whose bewildered expression almost made him laugh. "I don't know, Duncan. She's a hell of a marketing director. You'd be a fool to fire her."

Duncan shrugged. "If she's so great, she'll find another job."

"Sure she will. But it would be a shame to lose her. Say, isn't wasting resources a cardinal sin?" Gabe faced the door. "You could convince the owners they would be losing big if they let her go." He turned around in time to catch Duncan shaking his head.

"I'll see what I can do, buddy. You know 'saving' resources is not exactly my specialty, and not every business owner is committed to conservation—unless you're talking about dollars and cents."

Gabe continued through the door. "Sure, but I have faith in you. After all, sales *is* your specialty." As he continued toward his office, he hummed, his voice bouncing off the glass and brick and echoing over the lobby. He hoped Duncan's influence would echo through the company with equal force. If not, both Gabe and Fate could find themselves without a job.

Chapter Three
The unexpected sure makes life interesting.

Hoping for the best but expecting the worst, Fate doodled on a scrap piece of paper. She hated waiting on hold. Worse, she hated uncertainty, precisely what had inspired her call to the bank in the first place. But Carol, the mortgage representative, didn't appear to be overly pleased to hear from her.

Regardless, she needed to know the status of the mortgage. She'd passed Mr. Duncan in the hallway earlier, and he'd looked at her like she had three heads. She suspected he was waiting until after the presentation on Friday before politely offering her the choice of resigning or taking a demotion. Damn merger!

This phone conversation would determine her response.

Studying the dumpy desk and chair across the room, and listening to the recorded sales pitch on the telephone as she waited for Carol, she took note of his tacky accessories. A calendar with half-naked women draped over motorcycles, an obnoxious doll that sounded like Rodney Dangerfield, and a plush computer with long needles stabbed into it were scattered over his desktop. She could only imagine what his home must look like. No doubt decorated in typical bachelor pad fashion as his dorm room had been, cast-off furniture, hula dancer lamps, and beer signs plastered all over the walls.

They had precious little time to construct the new marketing strategy. He needed to get his butt in here, pronto.

Carol returned to the phone line and, in an unenthusiastic voice, apologized for making Fate wait so long. She then proceeded to explain to Fate that there'd been a delay. They were still waiting for the appraisal. The mortgage would not be going to committee for at least one week.

Fate's heart sunk. She hadn't bought a house before but had heard enough horror stories from friends to know things rarely went smoothly. The hope that her purchase would be an exception to the rule evaporated like spilled water in the desert. But then again, why should it go smoothly? What had she done to deserve that?

Considering the state of things in her life, why should she expect anything less than bedlam? She thanked Carol, hung up the phone, and rested her forehead in her hands, her elbows on the desktop. *Damn, damn, damn!*

"What's wrong? Looks like someone stole your puppy," Gabe said as he strolled into the room and shut the door.

"Nothing."

"Nothing, like really nothing? Or nothing like, 'I'm not going to tell you,' nothing?" He slumped into his chair with the grace of a dying dog.

Despite her frustration, she felt a smile tugging at her cheeks. Was he being intentionally silly, or was he simply a goof?

His eyebrows furrowed, he asked, "Now, what have you accomplished in my absence? After all, we are on a deadline."

Normally such a tone would have evoked a tirade, or in the least, a flood of defensiveness. But for some reason, she found Gabe's teasing manner distracting, even a little amusing. Why? Probably because if she didn't laugh, she'd cry.

Holding up her doodle pad to illustrate, she simply shrugged her shoulders. "I've managed to produce a remarkable likeness of a Hobbit, or," as she gazed at her scribbling, she continued, "possibly President Bush?"

He tsk-tsked as he gathered himself from his chair and strode across the room. Swiping the pad from her hands, he studied it. "Looks like I can't trust you to work independently. How in God's name you managed all this time without me—well, it's a wonder!" A silly grin had replaced his scolding grimace. "Nice study of contrasts, bold strokes...I'd say you've produced an amazing representation of the misery of the human condition—or a woman's more delicate anatomy. Can I have it?" He pulled off the top page.

She swiped it from him and crumpled it up. "You sick-o! Typical man. All you see in everything is sex."

"You expected anything different?" He dropped the pad on her desk and leaned down, until he was far too close for comfort. She could see flecks of gold in his gray eyes, an unexpected surprise. Had those been there years ago? Flashes of heat in cool depth. The air seeped from her lungs and she struggled to re-inflate them. What was her problem? Only this morning she'd hated this guy. He was stealing her job!

Six years. They'd battled for six turbulent, hellish years, the last three bumping into each other at Chamber of Commerce meetings and trade shows in downtown

Detroit, Chicago and Cincinnati. Their brief encounters had always been characterized by barely disguised insults.

He smiled, the expression genuine. Where was that pig-headed jerk she'd known for years? Had she really known him at all?

The question was ridiculous. Of course, she hadn't. How could she? Outside of that very brief stint in college, they'd spent very little time together and had recently talked about nothing deeper than the failure of another dating service, or the demise of each other's. But looking at him now, she had to wonder if, despite their new proximity, she would ever figure him out. His moods were more changeable than Michigan weather. One minute he was cocky and sarcastic, the next deep and introspective.

"How about 'Temptations'?" he whispered in her ear.

"What?" His question caught her off guard. What was he talking about? The silky tone of his voice and his penetrating gaze warmed her like she'd just eaten a tub of *jalapeño* peppers.

"The new name. Single Temptation."

"Oh." She wanted to giggle. She covered stinging cheeks with cool palms. What was he doing? Was he flirting with her? "Hmm. Pretty racy, don't you think? Might give people the wrong vibe."

"What's wrong with racy? We're dealing with younger clients, remember? They like racy. Sexy and fast, that's their world."

"Not all of them are that way. Are we targeting the fast crowd?"

He backed away, to Fate's relief. His cologne's scent— her favorite, Obsession—hung over her desk after he walked across the room. "I have an idea," he said, after gazing out the window for a moment. The sunlight flashed blue in his silky curls.

His gaze met hers, and she hesitated. There it was again. That crazy connection.

She couldn't speak, and she was afraid to ask about his idea. For some reason, she thought it might be dangerous. *Come on, Fate! This isn't college, and you're not the shy, self-conscious little mouse you used to be.* She prepared herself for the unexpected, or at least tried to. "Okay, what is it?"

"I still think we should find a game show to work with. Maybe the only way to learn whether or not that would work is to be a contestant."

She laughed, more from relief than anything else. That had been the last thing she'd expected him to suggest. "Me? On one of those shows? I don't think so. For one, I'm too conservative. And second, I'm too old."

Inspecting a print hanging on the wall, a fingertip tracing the frame, he asked, "You're far from old. What are you...twenty-three?"

"You're smooth."

He turned to face her. "Seriously, they take all types. I say we shoot for 'The Great Date,' it's local and could use some contestants."

"No way. You want to go for it, be my guest. But I don't want any part of it. With my luck, they'd pair me with someone absolutely insane—like you."

"Should I consider that an insult?" *That* look was pasted on his face, the one from college. The guy on the hunt, cocked eyebrow, lopsided smile. Appearing more than a little menacing, determined and in command...and very sexy, he stepped closer, and the cologne scent strengthened. As though the fragrance was some sort of intoxicant, it sent her heart palpitating.

"No, just a statement of fact," she said, hoping she sounded casual. She had to be going crazy. Why was she reacting this way? Why, why, why? She'd spent the last six years avoiding him, for God's sake!

He furrowed his brows, but mirth remained in his eyes. "Insane, eh? I was hoping for genius, quirky, fun, full of life, gorgeous, anything but insane. Guess I'd better work on it."

"Well, don't take my word on that. What do I know?" The conversation was getting too weird. If she didn't know better, she would think he was flirting. "Now, back to business. You go ahead, check out the game show. In the meantime, I'll do some research into the competition's names and see what I can come up with. We'd better start writing some things down." She pulled out a notebook. "Let's see. Target Market. Singles, ages twenty-one to forty."

She could feel him nearing, even though she was staring at the faint blue lines on the paper in front of her. Waves of electricity pulsed between them, sending heat to her skin and goose bumps down her arms again. The back of her neck prickled. Hot and cold. Was she getting sick? Probably the flu.

"Adventurous, active, fun-loving, seeking friendship or romance…"

She stopped writing. Was he still talking about their business plan?

"Why did you stop?" he asked from behind her. Smooth, chocolaty warmth emanated from him, seeping into the pores on the back of her neck and shoulders.

She better be getting sick.

"Sorry." She scribbled what he'd said and waited for more, grateful for the momentary silence. Her brain was on overload and she feared anything he said would end up jumbled beyond recognition. She rested a cool palm against her forehead and closed her eyes, willing her mind to clear.

A moment later, when the blood had returned to her brain, and she'd wrangled her reactive nerve endings into submission, she said, "Let's back up. What's our vision?"

"Hmmm. Good question." He rested a hand on her shoulder, sending those damn nerves into instant frenzy again. "I'd say it's to provide our clients with a unique and highly personal, oh—and successful service." There went the other hand on her other shoulder! *Double damn*! "So many dating services take your picture, film a video, or have you fill out a questionnaire then take your money and forget about you. I say we should take a more personable approach, follow up after dates, and of course, offer high quality applicants, based on sex, age..."

She shifted forward in her chair, knowing if he didn't get away from her right now, she'd go absolutely nuts. *Blah, blah, blah, blah, blah.* What had he said? She skimmed her notes, registering only one word. Sex.

He stepped away, fetched his chair and dragged it across the carpeted floor. He planted it next to hers and flopped into it, hanging over her back to read what she'd written. He was toying with her, he had to be. Her tongue felt swollen, and tiny droplets of sweat collected on her upper lip.

"Is there something wrong?" he asked after a few minutes.

"No. Nothing. I think I'm getting sick or something, so you might want to back up a bit."

"Sick, eh? That's too bad." He didn't sound sympathetic, and he didn't back away.

She glanced at her watch. "Oh, look. It's five o'clock. Time to go, bye." She slammed her notebook shut and stood.

"You're leaving early? I didn't think you ever did that. In fact, just this morning, I heard your old boss telling Duncan what a hard worker you are. How would it look if he saw you skating outta here at this hour now? Anyway, I was thinking we should grab some dinner on the company's tab, keep working. We have a lot to do and only nine more days to finish. One week from Friday's the day, Fate."

"How could I forget?" She sunk into her chair. He was right, even if he was manipulating her with that jab about Duncan. There was no way they'd get the plan finished in time if they didn't keep working. Duncan had essentially asked for a miracle, but she could understand why. What company could afford to sit idle for even one day? "Okay. Dinner first, or do you want to keep working for a while?"

Standing, he bowed like a gallant knight and held out his hand. "My lady, would you be so kind as to join me for dinner this eve?"

He was corny, but in a sweet way. What harm could there be in letting her guard down, if only a tiny bit, to see what Gabe Ryan was really all about? Oh no, this was dangerous thinking.

Okay, no need to panic yet. Should she go? No, she shouldn't go. Yes, she *had* to go. She just might learn what she needed to get him out of her office for good.

Then again, he might be trying to do the same to her. Well, well, well. Smooth isn't the word for you, Gabe Ryan, is it?

Chapter Four
It's no lie. Chemistry can be dangerous.

Just her luck! The only table in the crowded restaurant was one of those cozy corner booths where her knees constantly rubbed against the person's sitting next to her, Gabe, naturally. Her administrative assistant, Michael, sat on her other side, but his presence wasn't as settling as she'd hoped. Yes, it was a tiny help having someone else's face to look at, instead of being forced to stare at Gabe's gorgeous mug all night. But it didn't stop the rush of mind-melting heat every time Gabe's thigh brushed against hers, nor did it help her put together coherent sentences.

Oh hell! When had he gotten so good looking? Men got better with age, where women just drooped.

Definitely not fair.

"So, what do you think, Fate?" Gabe asked.

She hadn't heard the rest of the question, and if there was one thing she knew for certain, it was that she'd be a fool to answer any of his questions blindly. "What was that?"

Gabe shot a grin to Michael. "Told you."

"What? What are you guys up to?" She hadn't counted on them conspiring against her! Michael was so loyal.

Gabe's leg rubbed against hers again. This time it stayed put. When she tried to pull hers away, his moved with it.

Then a hand massaged her shoulder.

She felt like she was on a date. The scary part was, a big part of her wanted to snuggle up to the man...no, more than that, she realized when that knee stroked her outer thigh. She wanted to do much more than snuggle.

She wondered if the booth would become slick if she were naked, sweaty, with Gabe...*oh, hell!* "Would you two let me in on the joke?" She poked at her salad for the last time then shoved it aside. It was no use trying to eat.

Gabe gave her a sexy grin. "We were talking about work, of course." He shot Michael a conspiratorial look.

"Bullshit." She smacked his chest, and it took all the strength in her body to force her hand from him once it made contact. *Damn it! What's wrong with me? I don't need to revisit Gabe Land again. It's clearly no better a ride than it had been years ago...*

Speaking of ride...God, did he have a hard chest! She wondered if he was still as cut as he'd been in college. Back then he'd been a jock, his sport of choice, swimming. It was amazing what a little water did for a guy's body! His chest had been rock-hard and defined. His arms, too. Thick, defined, sexy. Classic washboard stomach. Every inch of that amazing body shaved smooth—Correction, almost every inch—Those inches spared by the razor were some of the best, too. *Damn it, get your mind out of the man's pants!*

"Actually," Michael said, "we were talking about the change in the brass. Gabe was telling me what a great boss

Duncan is. And I told him the green rug and polyester had to go."

Fate indulged in a giggle, stifled when that hand resting on her shoulder gave another little squeeze. What was that man trying to do to her?

Gabe chuckled. "Like I said, I've tried to tell him that some women find bald men sexy. What about you, Fate? Do you like bald men?" His gaze drilled her.

He was sitting too damn close...

He was too damn sexy...

That leg was rubbing hers...

Her mind was shut down. Permanently. "Uh. I need a drink." She searched the crowded room for the waiter.

Gabe flagged him down when he passed with a tray of frosty, foam-headed mugs of beer.

Yes, that's exactly what she needed. A cold beer. Ice-cold, to douse the warmth spreading over her crotch. Just dumping the stuff onto her lap might take it down a degree or two.

"You didn't answer the question," Michael said, giving Fate a poke. When had he become so uncharacteristically friendly? He was stiff, reserved, a damn good assistant. Not teasing, flirting, like he was acting now. "I can't stay away from them myself."

"Bald men?" she asked, wondering if she'd missed something again.

"Yep. They drive me crazy." He waggled his eyebrows.

Gay? Michael was gay? Why hadn't she known that before?

"Well, for some reason, I don't think that'll convince Duncan he needs to dump the rug. Last I checked he was straight."

Michael shrugged. "He's not my type anyway. I like 'em athletic."

Me too. "I can't say I go for the bald look. Guess it depends on the guy." She shifted, and the vinyl seat made an obscene sound. *Rpffffff.* Gabe raised an eyebrow and smirked. "It wasn't me. I mean it wasn't what you thought," she stammered.

Gabe smiled. "Sure, I believe you."

"Oh! Can we get some work done? That's why we're here, isn't it?"

The waiter set a tall lemon lager on the table, and she silently thanked him with a smile. She swallowed the icy liquid and felt the chill drift down to her stomach. Ah! Much better.

Gabe gave her a lopsided smile. A hand squeezed her knee.

So much for cooling off. More heat rocketed to her groin. Damn him! She crossed her legs and squeezed them closed against the tingle.

His fingertips traced circles on her knee. The circles moved slowly up, up, up until they reached the hem of her skirt, about midway up her thigh.

She chugged the rest of her beer then flagged down the waiter for another. Maybe a second one would do the job.

Gabe leaned forward, his chest and stomach resting against her back for one very long heartbeat. She felt herself leaning back into him.

This was not good!

He grabbed the new beer and took several gulps. She watched his throat work, and the lingering wetness glisten on his lips. She could lick that off.

"What about Single Temptation?" Michael said.

What were they talking about now? How had she lost track of the conversation?

"Single Temptation?" she repeated, trying to figure out what the hell they were discussing. There was a single temptation sitting next to her at the moment. One giant temptation...

"The new company's name," Gabe explained, licking a bit of foam from the corner of his mouth. "What you do think? Still too—uh, what did you say earlier? Racy?" There was another one of those wicked grins. He should be arrested for that! He was shamelessly propositioning her with his eyes. His gaze visibly drifted down her body then wandered back up to her face. "Is there something wrong with racy? Personally, I like it."

She brushed his hand off her thigh. "Like what? The company name or things that are racy?"

He set that mischievous hand right back where it had been, even a little higher. "Both, course that may be because I'm a little racy myself."

"I hadn't noticed." A smile pasted on her face for both men's benefit, she pried Gabe's hand from her leg and held it a safe distance away.

That was no better, especially when he tickled her palm with his thumb. She pushed, he pulled, she pushed again, he pulled.

Would he let her go, dammit?

He released her hand, and she sagged with relief.

Then he squeezed her thigh.

The man needed a straight jacket! And she needed another beer. Somehow that last one had disappeared, and she didn't remember drinking a bit of it.

The waiter brought her third lager and a fresh basket of nacho chips. She took a few, the salty taste a nice complement to the beer's fruity flavor.

"We already determined our niche audience." Gabe reached around her, lightly brushing the side of her breast as he scooped up a handful of chips from the basket. "I think we should use radio spots."

"No way. Too expensive," she said, dodging another accidental brush of his hand. "Are you insane? We'd spend our entire advertising budget in one month."

Gabe took her beer from her and swallowed half of it. "Then we need an angle to get free media."

Since when did he deserve to drink half her beer? Pig. "Would you quit doing that?"

"What? We're talking about work. What's wrong?"

"Quit drinking my beer. Get your own if you're thirsty."

"Sorry. I didn't think you'd mind sharing." The hand that had previously been holding her glass dropped back to her leg.

She wasn't sure which was worse, when it was delivering her beer to his mouth, or now, when it was delivering tingly heat to her crotch.

Oh boy, now was definitely worse! A fingertip traced her skirt's hem then slipped above it.

"You want to drink more? Be my guest. I think I've had enough." She shoved his hand away.

He chuckled and took up her beer, downing it in a few long gulps. "So, what about that angle? How can we get some free media?"

"How about some kind of scandal?" Michael offered. "Something newsworthy. Hey, should I take notes?"

"No, I'm sure we'll remember tomorrow," Fate said, trying like hell to stay in the conversation.

Michael reached down and took out a notepad from his briefcase then shot a smile in Gabe's direction. "I'll keep notes just in case."

"I don't think the new brass would appreciate us launching their new company by throwing dirt at the press," she continued, popping another chip in her mouth. She could feel a buzz spreading through her body. After what? One beer, and maybe a few sips of a second? She was such a lightweight when it came to drinking. Had always been. She wondered if Gabe remembered this.

"Then what about jumping into the spotlight with some other organization?" Gabe took another handful of chips from the basket and popped several into his mouth, then dropped that hand on her leg again.

Would he just give it up?

Did she want him to?

She brushed it away.

Gabe reached across the table, snagged Michael's notepad and read through the notes. Then he dropped it on the floor.

That had to be the saddest hanky-drop she'd ever seen! But that didn't stop Gabe from taking full advantage of it.

"I'm one clumsy jerk tonight. Sorry, Mike."

Michael visibly swallowed against the urge to correct Gabe about his name, and Fate started to laugh. But before she'd released more than one guffaw, a hand up her skirt, fingertips tracing the line of her thong, ceased all mirth. She felt her mouth hanging wide open and clamped it shut.

Did those fingers ever feel good!

He looked over his shoulder at her, stooped in a strange position as he supposedly groped for the lost notepad. His hand rested between her legs. "Are you all right? You look a little flushed."

"I'm fine. But I think you need to look elsewhere for the notes." She shoved his hand away. "Maybe we need to approach this from another direction."

"I'm listening." Gabe sat up, tossed the pad to Michael, and pressed against her.

Would he quit taking everything she said so literally? She looked at Michael.

"What direction, Fate?" Michael asked.

The faint trill of a cell phone sounded, and they each glanced down.

"It's mine." Michael punched the button and answered, stepping away from the table after a couple words.

Now she was left with Gabe. Alone. Oh, God!

He grinned at her like a cat might before it swallowed a canary. "Are you sure you're all right? You don't look so good. Do you want me to take you home?"

"I'm fine." She scooted away, hoping the distance might ease the heat between her legs.

"Have I told you how great it is working with you?"

"Indirectly."

He laughed, and she couldn't help admiring the way his features frolicked. A curl caught a breeze as the waiter swept by. She stopped herself before she reached for it.

"You're one hell of a woman, Fate."

"And you're one hell of a smooth talker, Gabe."

He grinned. "Actually, if you knew me better, you'd know I'm a straight shooter."

She didn't want to go there. For some reason talking about shooting anything left her head spinning. "I need to go to the bathroom." She grabbed her purse, scooted to the end of the bench, and stood, but immediately dropped back down.

The world was rocking under her feet like a moonwalk.

Guess I've had more beer than I thought, and how the hell had that happened?

"Are you all right?" Gabe was right next to her again.

"I'm fine. Just got a bad start the first time. I'll try again." She stood, and the world dipped and tipped. Her head swam. Two beers did that to her? Sheesh!

On legs that felt like they were tied to anchors, she slowly propelled herself through the crushing crowd to the bathroom. And after peeing a gallon, she checked herself in the mirror—not a pretty sight—and headed back to tell Gabe she needed to call it a night.

When she returned to the table, Gabe stood. "Ready to go?" he asked, car keys in hand.

"Yup. Where's Michael?"

"He left. Had a personal issue to deal with. Said he'd see you tomorrow." Gabe took her hand.

She sort of leaned into him as she walked. He didn't sway like the rest of the world did.

When she got to her car, she fished through her purse for her keys. When she hit the bottom, and still no keys, a tide of panic rose up her throat. "My keys! I must have lost them in the bathroom."

"I'll find them later. Why don't you let me drive you home?"

"No, all I need to do is go back inside." She took a step back toward the entry, but something caught her by the waist. "What the hell?" She looked down. Hands. She glanced over her shoulder. "Would you let me go?"

He spun her around until she was facing him directly.

Not a good position. He was so close. He smelled so good. He towered at least a head taller than her. Perfect height. Perfect width. Solid. Hard. Sexy...

He leaned down and dropped a kiss on her nose. "You're a very important part of the new Single Temptation. I couldn't let anything happen to you, now, could I?"

What?

"So, let's go to my car, and I'll drive you home." He didn't remove his hands from her waist.

"You're driving me home for the sake of the company?"

"Partly..." He glanced over her shoulder and smiled. "Okay, I confess. I'm worried about you for personal reasons. Don't you feel it, Fate? That old magic?"

"No." *Liar!*

His handsome face screwed into the picture of confusion. "Really?"

Actually, what she felt right now went way beyond what she'd felt in college. Had to be the Oregon lager. Probably had twice the alcohol content. "We have to work together, at least for the time being. We'd better keep things professional..." Her gaze dropped to his lips as he licked them, and she felt her own go Sahara Desert dry.

He leaned closer, and her eyelids fell closed.

His mouth touched hers, and an A-bomb exploded in her body. Shockwaves pulsed outward to her limbs and knocked her brain loose from its connections.

She wrapped her arms around his neck and held on for life, relishing the lazy, deliberate exploration Gabe was performing on her mouth. His fingers kneaded her waist then tiptoed up her sides. Hers tangled in silky curls at his nape.

By God, she'd lost her mind! But who the hell cared? He tasted amazing. He smelled wonderful. And as his body crushed against hers, he felt fantastic. Hard angles and planes. Smooth muscle working under clothes she wished she could strip away.

His hands found the sides of her breasts and slipped between their bodies to tease her nipples through her clothes. She could feel herself getting wet. She straddled his leg and ground into him in rhythm with the throbbing in her crotch.

She wanted him. Now! Her hands dropped to his hips and slowly slid around to his ass. Rock-hard! Something sharp poked her palm through his rear pocket, and in response to the pain, she slid her hands around to his front, grabbed the pronounced lump she found there and gave it a squeeze.

"Ouch!" Gabe broke the kiss and took her hands in his. "Easy, baby. This tool isn't a Craftsman. It needs a little gentle loving care. Eeeeasy does it."

The blinding white of a headlight flashed in her face, and she looked up into Gabe's face. "Oh. Sorry. Guess I got carried away." His mouth was still moist, hers sensitized. She licked her lips, still tasting him.

"Come on. Let's get outta here before we get a ticket." He took her hand and led her to a Corvette parked a couple of spots away.

Black, sleek, sharp. That vehicle was just like him, the epitome of racy.

"Nice car." She dropped into the passenger seat after he opened the door for her.

He went around to the other side. "It's a nice ride, but I'm about ready to turn her in for something better."

"What?" She fingered her mouth, still tasting him. "Maybe a Beemer next? Or a Ferrari?"

"No, I was thinking of something a little more practical. Like a truck."

"You? A truck?" She laughed at the vision of Gabe Ryan, bad boy, driving a dumpy old pick-up. "It'll never happen. Unless, of course, you buy one of those stupid trucks with five-foot tires."

He chuckled, started the car and shifted into drive. As he pulled onto the street she noted how smooth the ride was, indeed. She'd never ridden in a Vette before. It was kind of nice.

Within a few blocks, she'd rolled down the window, and was enjoying the exhilaration of a car that hugged the road and shot like a cannonball from the traffic lights. It might be fun to drive one of these, she decided.

The man might be as enjoyable to ride...assuming he'd taken care of that engine misfiring issue he'd had years ago.

When Gabe made a left at the next light, she realized he was taking her directly to her place.

Wait a minute. She hadn't given him directions. "How do you know where I live?"

"I, uh. I saw your personnel file on Duncan's desk earlier."

"Bullshit!" She went into her purse, pulled out her wallet and opened it. Her license was gone. "Where are my keys? My license?"

He parked the car in an empty parking lot, leaned to the left and slid a hand into his rear pants pocket. "Here." He dropped them into her lap. "I didn't want you to drive home."

"I'm fine."

"You didn't look fine."

"What do you care, anyway? Is this just your way of getting a little pussy? Act all honorable, drive the lady home, and then weasel your way into her house for a one-night stand." Damn, even to herself she sounded like a bitch!

"I promise I won't touch you again. I just wanted to drive you home."

She almost felt disappointed by that promise. "How am I supposed to get to work in the morning?"

"I'll pick you up."

He couldn't really be acting honorable. Chivalry was dead. Gone for centuries, at least since the advent of indoor plumbing. "What's in this for you?"

"Nothing. Like I said, I didn't want to see you get in a car accident. You're loaded, Fate."

"Am not."

"Sure. Then why are you swaying? We're not moving."

"Well..." Was she really swaying? She gripped the door handle to stop it just in case. "Then what are you doing taking advantage of me when I'm...I'm not at my best?"

"I promise," he held up his hands in the universal sign of surrender, "I won't touch you again."

Well, at least she hadn't lost her keys. That was a bit of a relief. The promise that he wouldn't try anything more wasn't, but it was late and it had been one hell of a day. She was probably lacking in mental facilities at the moment. Tomorrow, things would look different, and she'd be glad she hadn't done something stupid. "Drive on." She leaned back to enjoy the rest of the ride.

It took only a few minutes before they reached her house. Gabe insisted she wait for him to open the car door, and she relinquished. He was a bit old fashioned. She hadn't expected that.

When he opened the door, he offered a hand to her and she accepted, stepping from the low car's interior onto the tilty, wobbly sidewalk. He helped her to the door, helped her with the keys, assisted her inside and then stood at the threshold, looking like he was in pain.

"Thanks," she said, knowing exactly what kind of pain he was probably in. She was a hot, throbbing, mess too. Tonight, she'd need the company of Mr. Happy before she'd get any sleep. "You're a good sport, Gabe. I'm sorry for snapping at you. Like it or not, we have to find a way to work together, at least until Duncan fires me."

"He's not going to fire you."

"Yeah, yeah. Take his side." She slipped her feet out of her shoes. Ah! Her cramped toes wiggled, burrowing into the soft carpet. She dropped her purse and keys on the side table and reached up to let her hair—what remained in the ponytail—loose. She scratched at her scalp, bringing the blood flow back and sighed.

"Can you trust me?" he asked.

"No offense, but I don't trust anyone. Hell, I trusted my company—I was up for a promotion. They promised! Look what trusting them got me. Nowhere."

He nodded.

"My mother's house is going on the auction block soon, and I need to get a mortgage, or I can't buy it from the bank. I can't let my mother lose her house."

He leaned against the doorframe, looking casual, and extremely sexy. Arms crossed over that broad chest. "Is she still living in that tri-level in Canton?"

"She was." She shed her blazer and hung it on the back of her kitchen chair. "Before the bank kicked her out. You want something to drink?"

"No, thanks."

"How about something to eat? I have some munchies. I don't normally indulge—especially this late—but what the hell. I've broken a lot of rules today." While she was hidden in the confines of the kitchen, she quickly slipped off her pantyhose. Much better. Chips in hand, she returned to the living room.

"No, thanks." His gaze dropped to her bare legs, and he visibly swallowed. "Guess I'd better get going. I have a long drive home."

"You do?"

"Yeah. I moved out by the old Date Doctor's headquarters. It'll take me at least an hour to get home."

"Why don't you stay here?" Had she just said that? She bit her tongue.

"Oh, I don't think that would be such a good idea. Thanks anyway." He gripped the doorknob and gave it a twist.

"Are you sure? I mean, if you don't make it home tonight, I'll never forgive myself. You had a couple beers, too, you know."

"I'm fine. Unlike you, I ate my dinner. Really." He pulled the door open. "Besides, I'm sure you'd have a hell of a time sleeping tonight with me here."

"Aren't we a little full of ourselves?" She dropped the chips on the coffee table and sauntered to the door. Damn, she was feeling sexy tonight.

"No." He gave her a grin and one very long up-and-down twice-over then took a single step out the door. "I'm not full of myself. I'm just banking on the fact that you're not accustomed to having nude men sleeping on your couch." He winked. "See ya tomorrow morning, Fate. Seven sharp."

Nude? "Okay." Damn right she wasn't used to naked men on her couch! "But you need some coffee for the road. I insist." She pulled him back inside, shoved him toward the couch and then went to the kitchen to make the coffee. "Wait here. It'll only take a minute. It's the least I can do for all your trouble."

He looked amused.

"What?"

"This doesn't have anything to do with that naked comment, does it?"

"Hell, no!" *Liar!* "I just would hate to see you fall asleep at the wheel. Be right back." Once in the kitchen, she dumped some water and coffee grounds in their respective places then sat at the table to wait.

And wait…and wait…how freakin' long did it take for the coffee-maker to work? Was it broken? She lacked the energy to get up and check on it. No, it couldn't be broken. It was brand new. She rested her arms on the table and dropped her head onto them…and fell asleep.

It was pretty quiet in the kitchen, and still no nutty coffee aroma. Time to check on Fate.

He walked around the half wall separating the living room from kitchen.

Sleeping. He wasn't surprised. And quite a picture, she was, too. Her red curls falling across her face and shoulders. Her features relaxed, lacking the tension he'd seen all day. She looked younger, innocent, vulnerable…and a little uncomfortable. She'd have one hell of a stiff neck tomorrow if she didn't move.

He shook her shoulders, and she groaned. He called her name, and she moaned. Still, she didn't move.

Well, he couldn't leave her there! Hell, she might slide sideways and crack her head on the floor. He scooped her into his arms, loving the feel of her weight against him. His cock got harder than concrete. Wishing she were wide awake, begging for his touch, he set her on the bed.

That was better. He took a step back, his gaze resting on her form. She still didn't look very comfortable. Had to be the belt. That was it. He removed it, receiving a soft sigh as a reward.

Hmmm...her blouse and skirt looked a little restricting too. What kind of gentleman would he be leaving her like this when she was so helpless? He sat next to her on the bed, playing with a flame-colored curl twisting around his fingertip. Undressing her was not an attempt to excise his libido. Not at all. She was loaded, couldn't undress herself, and uncomfortable. And he could help her, poor baby. He was being...chivalrous. Yeah, that was it.

He started with the jacket, not an easy task, since it was cut to fit and clung to her shoulders like a possessive boyfriend. But after some interesting and rather comical maneuvers, he managed well enough. He hung it on the doorknob—would hate to see it get wrinkled.

Next came the blouse. That was an altogether different kind of challenge. With each button released, his cock became harder until he could just about holler. Her smooth ivory-skinned stomach, concave and about as tempting as a cold beer on a hot summer day, was fully exposed, as was her sexy black lace bra. What a combination! Short black skirt and lace bra to match. Too bad she couldn't come to work dressed like that!

He could even see the pink of a lonely nipple peeking through the lace. It needed a kiss.

He bit his lip. Damn it, he wanted to taste her! Just one lick.

But how chivalrous would that be?

He sighed, frustrated, nursing a set of blue balls, and forced himself to finish the job. He had to reach around her back to unzip her skirt, and that left him painfully aware of how she smelled, how she felt in his arms, how soft her skin was and how sweet she was rumpled and sleeping. With a groan, he unzipped her skirt, stood at the foot of the bed, turned his head and pulled.

He wouldn't look. That would be the end of him.

Okay, maybe just one tiny look.

Holy shit! Black lace thong? His gaze riveted there, at the black V between her legs, then wandered upward.

She smiled in her sleep and rolled onto her side, jutting that delectable ass out. Black lace disappeared between two round, firm cheeks. He could touch them. He could bite them. He could do a lot of things to them.

But damn it all, he wouldn't! At least not tonight.

Time for a cold shower.

Chapter Five
*Mothers always know the most
inopportune times to call.*

The next morning, a mild hangover was the least of Fate's regrets. Sure, she hadn't done much with Gabe...at least she didn't think she had. Last she remembered she'd kept her clothes on. But waking up completely—okay, almost—naked was a big surprise. The kind of shocker that sends a person running for the bathroom to check things out. She hadn't been that drunk last night, had she? Surely she'd remember if they'd fucked!

Then again, maybe the dreams still fresh in her mind hadn't been dreams at all...

Shit! She checked her whole body for signs of lovemaking, love bites, anything. Finding nothing, she showered, dressed, and waited for Gabe to pick her up for work, the whole time a pleasant ache pulsing between her legs.

He'd undressed her. That thought alone turned her on.

She stretched away a bit of stiffness in her neck and gazed out the living room window. Still no Gabe. She glanced at the clock. Seven-twenty. Where was he? Had he forgotten? Was he feeling so rotten for what he'd done last night—which was nothing, she guessed—that he couldn't face her today?

She stared at the street, somewhat comforted when she spied the sexy black car prowling toward her driveway. In one swoop, she grabbed her purse, briefcase, and lunch and headed for the door, meeting Gabe on the front porch.

He smiled. "Morning. How're you feeling?"

"I'm okay. Swallowed half a bottle of Tylenol, but otherwise, I think I'll live."

"You did?"

"I'm kidding. Honest."

He glanced at his watch. "Sorry I'm late."

"It's okay. At least I won't be the only one late to work."

"We won't be late. Promise." He dropped behind her as she walked, a hand resting at the small of her back. The seemingly innocent contact sent her heart into a wild gallop.

"There's another one of those promises," she teased, glancing over her shoulder as she dropped into the passenger seat. Her gaze was met with a very warm one in return.

"I kept my word last night."

"You did?" Guess she had her answer, sort of. "I mean, yes, you did." A smidge of disappointment settled in her gut. She watched him walk around the front of the car, and heat spread through her body as he slipped into the seat next to her. His hand gripped the stick shift as he shifted into reverse and backed out of the driveway. She watched him orchestrate the movement of legs and hands as he drove. "I've never driven a stick. Is it hard?"

"Depends upon how you grab it. Wanna check for yourself?" He motioned toward his lap.

She rolled her eyes, hoping to hide her sudden case of guilt for manhandling his 'stick' last night, and smiled. "Seriously."

He sighed. "Just a little tricky at first. Some cars are harder, only because the clutch can be difficult to press in. This car's a breeze to drive."

She nodded and watched familiar houses drift by as they neared the main road. "Thanks again for driving me home last night. You were right. I guess I wasn't in any condition to drive."

"No problem. There's no way I'd let a friend drive like that."

"So, we're friends now?"

He glanced at her. "You mean we weren't before?"

She laughed. He was such a knucklehead. A delightful, funny, sexy goof. "Not in my book."

"Damn! You were on my Christmas card list."

She chuckled. "Then why didn't I get a card this past Christmas?"

"I didn't send anyone a card. I'm terrible with those kinds of things. Someday, when I get married, my wife'll have to handle that, or we'll be disowned by our friends and family for sure."

The picture of him married with a house full of kids sent another chuckle into her throat. "You? Married?"

"Hey, it could happen." He stopped at a red light and gave her a heart-stopping smile. "You don't think I'm marriage material?"

"Not at all." *Maybe* prime beef for a nighttime romp...

"Why's that?" He shifted the car into gear and it rocketed away from the intersection, leaving the other cars behind in the dust.

"You're too racy, just like your Vette."

"It's all show."

She studied his profile, wondering if he was telling her the truth, or just telling her what he thought she might like to hear. "I don't believe that for a minute."

"Well, then I'll just have to prove it to you. I think I'm headed in the right direction. Last night, for one, should give you at least an inkling. You passed out cold. I could have stayed at your place, stripped naked, and probably gotten some—"

A current of heat shot to her face, and a few rivulets wandered down to her belly. "Whoa! What are you talking about?"

"I know you wanted it. No use denying it."

"What I wanted had nothing to do with the *it* you're thinking of."

Gabe shook his head. "I guess I had you pegged wrong. I didn't think you were the kind to deny your own sexuality. Thought you were a little more aware than that."

Her face couldn't get any hotter. She turned from him and rested ice-cold fingers on her flaming cheeks. "I am *aware*."

"Then why lie?" He stopped the car at another red light. And as she glanced at him, she caught his gaze wandering over her form. Slow and lazy, yet intense at the same time. It was the kind of gaze a man gave a woman when he wanted "some."

And it was working…

She crossed her legs, imagining how he would feel resting between them. She loved the weight of a man, solid and hot, on top of her.

Her mouth went dry. Her heart pounded in her ears. That familiar throb settled in her crotch. Damn it! How would she work like this?

"Can we talk about something else?"

He drove away from the light, and she was grateful when she spied the building up the street. "Sure."

Thank God!

They pulled into the parking lot, and Fate retrieved her purse, briefcase, and lunch from the floor before stepping from the car. She made a beeline for her office, noting the unfamiliar face at the reception desk in the lobby.

Damn it! She'd forgotten about Julie. In her place at the Chrome Throne stood a blonde with boobs that had to have set her back at least ten grand and a face that had to cost her at least double that. Fate nodded a greeting at the woman and headed upstairs, listening to Gabe's animated voice behind her.

Evidently, Gabe knew Miss Plastic Surgery.

Why did that bother her so much?

Up above, she stood on the balcony and watched him chatter with the woman. She really was gorgeous, in that Baywatch blonde bombshell sort of way.

Racy. That woman was racy.

Gabe said he liked racy.

She bumped into something with her shoulder. She turned.

Michael smiled at her. "Morning, Fate. How're you feeling?"

"I'm fine."

"I had a great time last night. We should do it again sometime."

"Sure."

"Well, gotta go. I've got a ton of work to catch up on."

"What work?" She hadn't given him anything since last week, and with the company change, those reports wouldn't be needed.

"Gabe gave me some things to follow up on. I have a list." He waved a manila file at her.

"He did?" When had he found the time? Was he already trying to show her up? "What kinds of things?"

"Just some market research stuff. Competitors and such."

"Okay. Just do me a favor. Give me a copy of everything when you're done."

"Will do, Fate." He hurried toward the stairs, catching Gabe at the bottom.

Fate watched them talk. Couldn't make out a word. She'd never make it as a lip reader.

What was Gabe up to? Trust him? Her ass! There wasn't one single cell in Gabe Ryan's body that deserved to be trusted.

She went into her office and took a seat, dropping her head back and closing her eyes for a moment. Her neck and shoulders were stiff as hell, already, and her head was pounding. The painkiller wasn't doing a bit of good.

"You're not feeling so hot, are you?" Gabe asked as he entered.

She didn't bother opening her eyes. "I'm fine."

"You're a bad liar."

She listened to his footsteps approach. As each one grew closer, her nerve endings prepared for the shock of his touch. Where would it be?

Her shoulders.

At first she flinched. But as he kneaded the sore muscles like a pro, she started to relax. "Oh...yeah..." She groaned. She moaned. "God, that feels good."

"Just relax, trust me. I took a class or two, wanted something to fall back on if the marketing gig fell through."

"You wanted to be a massage therapist?"

"Sports trainer, actually."

She opened her eyes, and he smiled down at her.

This was not a comfortable position. With her head flopped back, she had no choice but to meet his gaze, and that gaze was mighty hot. Then it dropped a little and she found herself looking down to see what he was staring at.

Her shirt—correction, her chest. From his vantage he had a nice view of rounded cleavage miraculously enhanced by her black lace Wonder Bra. "Like what you see?" She raised an eyebrow.

"Sure do." He licked his lips. "What's not to like? Two firm, round breasts, just the perfect size to—"

"Okay, Hound Dog, off!" She shrugged her shoulders and slumped forward, temporarily out of his reach. "I need to get to work."

"Sorry." He stepped away, and she felt a chilly cloud settle around her. He slumped into his chair, his back to her.

Peace. At last. So, why did she feel so rotten? Why did her legs itch to carry her over to that tippy desk? Why was only one thing on her mind?

What had he done? Hypnotized her?

She spent the rest of the morning shifting papers from one folder to another, and doodling on her note pad. Didn't accomplish a single thing. Nadda.

This was not going to work! She'd be staring at a pink slip in less than a week if she didn't get her act together. Pronto. At lunch time, she passed Duncan in the corridor. He gave her an empty smile and asked her how the new arrangements were working, but he didn't stick around long enough to hear her answer.

Yep, she would have that pink slip by next Friday at the latest.

Gabe disappeared at lunch—probably had a friendly meal with Miss Plastic Surgery—so she ate alone at her desk.

Alone. Lonely. Funny, in one day he'd turned her life upside down. The office felt empty, lifeless, too silent. She used to always eat alone at her desk before. It hadn't felt lonely then.

He returned on the hour, flush-faced. Had he...? Oh, she didn't want to know. For some reason, imagining his hands on that...that fake woman with Pamela Anderson lips and boobs...grrr!

Why was she jealous?

He returned to his desk, spun his chair around and crossed his arms over his chest. "Have you had enough silence for a while? If I have to sit here for another four hours without speaking, I'm going to chew right through this desk." He looked so utterly charming, basically pleading with her to talk to him. What an odd character! A curl flopped over his forehead, striking a spark in her belly. Damn, he was cute.

"Yes, I've had enough silence."

"Good." He jumped from his chair and was at her side in two long strides. He returned to massaging her shoulders. "How's the hangover? Gone yet?"

She closed her eyes, lost in the sensations pummeling her. The smell of his cologne. Yum! The way his fingers put just the right amount of pressure on her tense muscles. The growing tingle between her legs.

What had he asked? "Mmmm..." was all she could muster.

"Guess that means it's gone." He moved up to her neck, fingertips walking up and down both sides. "Feel good?"

She slumped her head forward. "Yeah."

He worked his way down, easing her over her desk until her chest was pressed against the top, her arms crossed, her forehead resting on her wrists. With nothing but the feel of her slick desktop, cold, and unyielding under her arms, and his hands on her back, massaging away the tension she hadn't realized was there, it wasn't long before she was completely turned on.

She'd never had sex in the office before...

The desk was probably the perfect height...

What was she thinking?

She sat up. "That's great. Thanks!" The ache between her legs was almost unbearable, and the once cold desktop was doing nothing to cool her off. She was hot from toes to hair roots, and everywhere in between.

When had she become such a sensual creature? Her last boyfriend had complained incessantly about her lack of sexual response, and she had to admit she'd been a cold fish. She'd even considered going to a doctor to see if she needed those pills—the female version of that little blue one.

Guess it hadn't been a hormonal thing! That was a relief.

"Do you want to work together?" he asked as he dragged his chair across the room. He parked it next to hers and dropped into it. "We were off to a good start last night."

We sure were! The first image that came to mind was that moment in the parking lot. His hands on her breasts, his mouth exploring hers. "Where do you want to start?"

He leaned close. His mouth was right there. All she had to do was lean...just a little, a little more... His breath brushed her mouth. Her lips went dry, and she licked them. They didn't touch his, almost. She waited for him to close the hair's-breadth distance between them.

Without moving that gorgeous mouth, he reached around her and slid her doodle pad across the desk. "How about listing options for media?" he whispered.

How could he think about work?

"To hell with that." She cupped his face in her hands and took control, kissing him like she meant it. Her lips massaged his. Her tongue ran along the seam of his lips and begged admission. He opened to her, and her self-control snapped. Her tongue danced with his, a riotous tango, thrusting in and out. Her body ached for completion, and she turned her chair, stood and straddled his legs. He held her ass as she sat on his lap, her skirt hiked high over her hips, her legs spread wide.

Damn! She ground herself into him, ever aware of his erection through his clothes. Her hips gyrated, the rhythm slow and sexy. She felt his hard-on through her nylons and soaked satin panties.

He broke the kiss. "Better close the blinds, eh?"

She looked over her shoulder at the wide window, open to the balcony outside, and a matching one across the way on the other side of the lobby. No one was out there, and she was suddenly grateful for the fact that her office sat at the very end, thereby inviting very little passing foot traffic. Still, if the lights were on—which they were— anyone standing on the balcony across had a clear shot into her office. And who was housed in the office directly across from hers?

Duncan.

"You don't think he saw us, do you?"

"No, he's gone for the afternoon."

She sagged with relief then stood and dropped the blinds over the window. When she spun around to face him, he was looking at her, expectation written all over those picture-perfect features.

A tiny part of her hesitated. He was so sexy, so unbelievably good looking. And it felt so right being in his arms. But, they were working together. What would this do to her ability to concentrate? Now, more than ever, she needed to simplify her life, remove distractions, focus on what was important.

He raised a brow. "Are you sure about this?"

"No, I'm not."

"Then we won't."

"But…" This was so hard to talk about. "I'm horny as hell. What you do to me!"

He chuckled and took her in his arms. "You know what you do to me, too. But I can wait until you're ready."

"I was ready before…" She was very aware of the slick wetness in her panties. It felt cool as she moved.

"We have time. No need to rush." Holding her close, he rested a palm against the side of her head, and she closed her eyes and listened to the steady thump of his heart.

"I just can't believe we're even thinking about this."

With a finger under her chin, he forced her to look up. "Why not? We were amazing together. Have you forgotten?"

She had, if it had been this good. "No. Uh. I just remember you being a little quick. I'm sorry, that was spiteful. What I do remember was the constant bickering."

"That's changed. We're getting along fine and now I like to take things slow. I'm not that boy anymore. I'm all grown up. I've learned the value of…patience." He dropped a kiss on her nose then trailed more over her eyes, down her hairline, and up and down the side of her neck. Goose bumps blossomed over one arm, and she shivered. "You don't remember this?"

"No, remind me."

He reached a hand and teased her nipple through her shirt then unbuttoned one, two, three buttons. He bent lower and kissed the crest between her breasts. "Damn, you're so beautiful. Absolutely perfect. The way you look. The way your body responds to my touch. The way your lips form that special smile, just for me."

She leaned back, grateful her desk was behind her to stop her from falling to the floor. Her head dropped back, her eyelids closed. He pulled her bra aside and blew on her nipple, bringing it to instant hardness. That wasn't enough, though. He nipped it, teased it with his tongue and mouth until the throbbing between her legs had returned full force.

She tangled her fingers in his silky curls, welcoming his onslaught on her breast, and grateful when he moved to the other side.

"Let me refresh your memory." He teased that nipple to aching erection then finished unbuttoning her shirt, trailing kisses down her stomach. He reached around and grabbed her ass, lifting her up and setting her on the desktop.

He looked at her through heavy-lidded eyes and slid his hands up her skirt. One palm settled over her mound, rotating slowly until she thought she might come then and there. Her eyelids fell closed.

"I couldn't forget," he said. "For years, I've remembered the way you look, smell, taste." His fingertips caught the waistband of her nylons and panties, and she lifted her hips to allow him to pull them off. He slipped her shoes back on after tossing the clothing aside. "High heels are incredibly sexy."

She felt sexy. Sexier than she'd ever felt. The way he looked at her! She might as well be the most perfect woman in the world.

"Can I taste you?" he asked, stooping down and kissing her ankles. He licked and nipped the sensitive skin behind her knees then moved higher to her thighs. "Can I taste all of you?"

Her legs parted. "Oh, yes! Feast away." The only thing she could think about was having him inside. Her body thrummed with the thought. Every nerve ending pulsed. "I want you."

"Are you sure?"

"Yes."

He pushed her skirt up to her waist and eased her legs apart, devouring her with eyes flashing hot with need. "My God, look at you. So wet and ready for me." He inhaled. "And that scent. There's nothing like the smell of a woman. My woman."

Her arms trembled as she leaned back on them. And when the first touch of his tongue came, they nearly turned to marshmallows.

Electric shocks shot up her spine.

He started slowly, laving her folds then parting them and making tiny circles over her clit. A finger slipped inside, stroking the sensitized walls as his tongue lapped her clit with a steady motion that carried her closer and closer to completion.

She mentally tried to resist coming. But her efforts were failing miserably. He was so good. He knew where to touch. He knew exactly how fast, how much pressure... She was in heaven.

When that telling flush shot up to her face, she pushed his head away. "Stop."

He smiled. "What's wrong?"

She swallowed a cotton ball that had settled in her throat. "I need you inside me. Now."

"Then take me." He stood up and spread his arms wide. "Do what you will."

The phone rang, and they both looked at each other then at the intrusion.

Damn it to hell!

Thank you, God!

She closed her legs, yanked her skirt down and scooped up the receiver. "Fate Doherty."

"Hello, Honey? It's Mom. Are you busy right now, or can you talk?"

Shooting Gabe one of the most genuine silent apologies she'd ever had to give, she scooted down from the desk and wriggled by him. Breathless, she scooped up her panties and hose from the floor and flopped into her chair. "I can…talk. What's up?" she stammered.

"Dear, are you all right? You sound out of breath."

She swallowed and tried to force her breathing to slow. "I'm fine."

"You should take a vitamin with iron. You know how easy women can become anemic."

"Mother. I'm not anemic. I just…er, ran up the stairs. Why did you call?"

"Stairs, hmm? I just wanted to see how you're doing, that's all." Translation, did she have the mortgage yet.

"I'm doing fine, Mom. Still don't have word from the mortgage company."

"Well, they're taking a mighty long time. Don't you think?"

Gabe was sitting in his chair watching her. She smiled at him, mouthing, "sorry."

He shrugged his shoulders and lifted his fingertips to his nose then grinned.

A bolt of heat shot down to her crotch.

"...and you know the auction is scheduled for only two weeks from now." Her mother continued. "What am I going to do? You have to help me."

"Don't worry. I'm doing everything I can. We'll figure something out. Promise."

"Okay. Well, I have to go. Bye, honey."

"Bye, Mom." She dropped the phone in the cradle. "You're evil!" She gave him a playful pat on the stomach.

He caught her wrist. "What was that all about?"

"My mother. I told you about her house, didn't I?"

His thumb stroked her wrist, the simple touch a huge distraction. She glanced down at his hand.

"You did. That's right. Something about buying the house from the bank, right?"

"I was able to talk them into letting me buy it, but they gave me a set date, and if I don't come up with the money, they will put it on the auction block." She pulled her wrist free. It was simply too hard to concentrate when he was doing that thumb rubbing thing. "I'm running out of time. Fast."

"How much money do you need?"

"One twenty-five."

"Not bad for a four bedroom in Canton!"

"Yeah, it's a steal. I can hardly afford to lose this opportunity, even if it hadn't been my childhood home. But I'm having a hard time getting a mortgage. My credit's shot, thanks to some really stupid mistakes I made about six months ago." She looked down at her desk and slid a hand to her doodle pad. She swiped a pen out of the holder and started drawing little circles. "Sometimes I just don't think."

"I've made some stupid mistakes, too."

"*The* perfect Gabe Ryan make a mistake? No way!" She looked up and caught a playful smile.

"You'd be surprised. Like I said, you don't really know me. I've grown up since college."

"I'm glad to hear that." Their gazes locked, and an awkward silence dropped between them. Her heart pounded in her ears. After a few rather long moments, she added, "Well, should we get something accomplished today?" *Besides soaking my panties.*

"Sure. I've got Michael digging up some facts on our competitors, I hope you don't mind."

Was he being straight with her? She studied him as he stood and rummaged through several folders on his desk. She really wanted to believe him, wanted to trust him. "No, not at all. For now, I guess we're sharing both an office and an assistant."

"For now." He returned to his chair, cocking his head like a puppy. "What?"

Her neck flamed. "Sorry. Was I staring?"

"Yeah. Is something wrong?"

What wasn't wrong? She couldn't make up her mind about this guy. Her body had one notion—and only one! That was as puzzling as the rest of the situation. "I'm just not sure what to think about all of this. Only a few days ago, you were my worst enemy, and now…" What could she say about him? What was he? Almost her lover? The man she wished she could toss on the floor and ride like a wild stallion?

He gripped her upper arm, not hard. Just hard enough to capture her attention. "What, Fate? What am I to you?"

She shook her head. "I don't—"

"Bullshit." His gaze pummeled her, intense, relentless, fixed.

"What am I to you?" she asked, unable to tear her gaze from his.

"You're the woman I've loved...for six years."

Chapter Six
*Sometimes, a simple three-word
sentence can change your life.*

Well, that was something he hadn't thought to tell her, at least not yet. Still gripping her arm, Gabe waited, his breath caught somewhere between his lungs and his throat. Would she laugh in his face?

She didn't laugh. She did something worse. "I didn't...oh, my God...I, uh..."

"Pretty damn surprising, isn't it?" he summed up for her, releasing her arm. "You thought I was a player, right? On to the next one after you dumped me, right?"

She shrugged and took a step backward. "Well, it's been a long time. And we were so young."

"Maybe. But not me. I loved you, Fate."

She looked sick. Pale, weak, her shoulders slumped forward. She slid down in her chair. "I'm sorry."

Uh, uh! Gabe Ryan didn't appreciate pity, especially from Fate. He would rather have her hate him than pity him. Anger looked damn good on the woman. She wore it with such class and style. Shoving aside the sketch pad, he sat on her desktop. "For what? What are you apologizing for?"

"For the crappy way I treated you, I guess."

He leaned closer, drawn by her cologne. The slight tang tickled his nose. It was damn sexy. Not at all the sticky sweet fragrance she'd worn years ago. "Don't apologize for that. You did me a favor."

"Really?" She sat a little taller, a small improvement, but an encouraging one.

"Sure. You set me straight." He scooped up her sketch pad and flipped the pages, finding a caricature of himself with wild hair, blown up muscles, and a screw-the-world expression on his face. He wasn't surprised she still saw him that way. "I know why you dumped me in college. I learned a lot about myself over the past six years. I've done a lot of growing up. Made a lot of changes. Done a lot of soul-searching."

She tugged at the sketch pad, but not hard enough to wrestle it away from him. "You have?"

"Yep."

"Then why did you act the way you did with me? Whenever we bumped into each other...you were such a jerk."

He leaned closer, knowing he always got to her when he did that. "Was I?"

This was no exception. She bit her lip, a lip he knew tasted like honey. A lip he wished he could kiss right then... His cock hardened. "I guess it was me."

He released the pad, dropped his gaze to her chest, and visually feasted on the swell of two perfect tits bound in a black lace bra. "Sometimes we see what we expect to see."

She stood and buttoned her shirt. Damn! He'd hoped she wouldn't do that. That cleavage was simply too delicious to cover. "I don't know. All of this is so much to take in." She gripped her panties and pantyhose in her hand and headed toward the door. "What are you doing here now?"

Trying like hell to get you back in my bed where you belong. "My job."

She leaned back against the door, and he briefly considered pinning her there, gripping that ass in his hands, and lifting her high, impaling her on his rock-hard cock.

"Then you *are* competing with me for the marketing position."

He took a couple steps toward her. "No. I want to work together. I told you that."

"But Duncan said they don't need two managers." Looking completely confused and flustered, not that he could blame her, she shifted her weight from one foot to the other.

He took another step closer. "Screw Duncan. I think if we do a good job together, he'll keep us both. I know him. Know the way he ticks."

"What about the other VP's? You know them too?"

"Most of them." He took another step closer, but stopped mere inches away. His arms ached to enclose her, keep her safe and warm. He wanted to take care of her, even though he knew her pride would never allow it. "You don't need to worry, Fate. Trust me. Can you? You'll keep your job, buy your mother's house, and live happily ever after."

She chuckled. "Yeah. Just like that. Sorry, Mr. Fantasy, but real life is never that simple—at least not my life."

"But have you ever tried living by faith?" When she scoffed, he added, "Seriously."

"Of course I have. And now I'm facing the consequences, like all grown-ups do."

He shifted his weight forward, catching himself with outstretched arms, his palms flat on the door, on either side of her head. He inhaled her scent, and his cock tugged against his pants. "Really? Like when? What have you believed in? What do you believe in?"

She tipped her chin up. "Well, I believe in...in...myself."

He let his arms bend, bringing his body closer to hers. "Yeah? That's a start."

She nodded. "It's a hell of a start." She shook her head. "Wait a minute! A start? What do you mean by that?"

He stooped a little, bringing his face in line with hers. Her mouth was so moist, so sweet, so close. "I'm not trying to insult you."

"Since when did you get so deep, buddy? Last we dated, the deepest conversation we had was over whether to go for pizza or Chinese."

"See? I have changed. I'm nothing like I was in college."

"You're trying too hard to convince me. Why are you doing this?" She rung her pantyhose in her hands, and he wondered if she'd be able to put them back on after she was done with them. Then again, she looked fantastic without them.

"I can stop." He stepped back and motioned toward her twisted nylons. "Are you going to put those things on so we can get back to work? We have a lot to do, remember?"

The muscles along her jaw tightened, and he swallowed a chuckle. It gave him so much pleasure setting her off. Bad, but fun. He didn't know if he'd ever be able to give that up completely. He could picture himself teasing her years from now, when they were old and gray, stationed in their respective La-Z-Boys in front of the TV, watching round-the-clock game shows.

What a vision! Simple, maybe stupid, but that was all he wanted. A future with Fate, and a chance to grow old together.

And he knew in his gut he was at least two steps closer to it than he had been just a couple of days ago. Yep, things were going his way.

Before the end of next week, Fate Doherty would see things in a whole new light. Guaranteed!

She stomped out of the room, and he ruminated over the situation while she was gone. He wanted her. He loved her. She had no idea what she wanted, how great a catch he was.

What would make her appreciate him? Hmmm…

An idea started forming in the back of his head. What if? What if…she went out with another guy…? He hated the idea already, but he continued to follow the train of thought. It was best to play each idea out first before making a decision.

He could call it research. She'd learn what kind of guys were out there, and learn to appreciate him more.

The idea had merit. It could work. It could blow up in his face, too. But the reward was worth at least a little risk.

She returned, nylons in place. And panties, too, he assumed. *A shame.*

"I have an idea."

She stiffened then sat at her desk. "What idea?"

"I think we should do a little investigating. Check out the competition. How about we pick a dating service and let them set us up on a date? See where their strengths and weaknesses are. It's done in other industries, might help us find our slant. What do you say?"

She grimaced. "A date?"

"You can pick the service. You got a phone book? Let's see what we can find."

"I don't know about this." She spun her chair around and bent down to retrieve the Yellow Pages from a bottom shelf.

He leaned over a little to catch a glimpse of leg. Very nice. If they both lived to be one hundred, he'd never get enough of those legs. He prepared to right himself before she caught him. "Oh, come on! It's for our company. What could possibly happen?" Oops. Too late.

She eyed him speculatively, but didn't fight the smile blossoming over that perfect mouth. "The guy could be a lunatic."

"What's the chance of that? Slim to none? Hell, you work with a lunatic. We get along fine."

She chuckled. "You have a point."

He forced himself to look at the listings. "How about 'Let's do Lunch?' That one sounds pretty tame."

"Okay. I guess I can handle a lunch date." She didn't sound convinced.

He glanced up. She didn't look thrilled either. Yep, this could definitely work to his benefit. "I'm sure they screen their applicants. You'll be meeting in a public place.

You never know, maybe you'll even enjoy yourself." *She'd better not! I'll kill the bastard.*

She tipped her head. "I doubt it." Her eyebrows furrowed. "So, are you okay with this? I mean, moments ago you told me you loved me. And we've been...well, you know." Her cheeks turned a sexy shade of pink. The color washed down her neck and plunged below the V of her white shirt's neckline. The image of those luscious breasts lying just beyond that opening shot through his mind and left his trousers snug around his hips.

Damn hard-on! He had one almost constantly when he was in the room with her.

"I'm fine." He shifted in his chair. "For one, we're doing this in the interest of work. Second, if you don't share my feelings, then I can't stake a claim to you, can I? And third, it's only lunch. I doubt one lunch date will lead to much more than swapping small talk." *Damn better not! I'll kill him. He better not touch her, look at her, admire her...poor schmuck. He doesn't stand a chance.*

She nodded. "That's very big of you. I mean, we aren't officially dating or anything, but we've done a lot recently...I mean, some guys would assume we're dating. And they'd get jealous. Maybe you have grown up a little. I respect you for that."

Hey, what'd you know! It's working already. All right! He donned his version of Mr. Humble. "Well, I wasn't trying to impress you or anything, but if I did, I'll take it."

She smiled. Damn, did she have a great smile! It was a traffic stopper for sure. She could do movies.

Maybe they'd make a movie or two later... He'd never made home porn before, but he had a video recorder. He wondered if she'd play along. Her naked on film...

There went that hard-on again!

"Have you ever been in a movie?" He jotted down the dating service's phone number so he could call from his cell. Assuming the service had caller ID, he didn't want them to see where he was calling from.

"No, why?" She looked up at him, her face the picture of curiosity.

"Just wondering. You have a great smile."

That sexy pink color washed over her face and neck again. He longed to open that shirt to see where the blush ended. Someday he'd find out. Someday soon. "Really?"

He nodded then went back to his desk to retrieve his cell phone. "Shall we?"

"Okay." She swept up her own, and they each dialed the number and booked an appointment. She punched the call button on her phone long before he did. "Well?"

"My appointment's at six tonight. You?"

"Five-thirty."

He glanced at his watch. "We have a couple hours. Do you want to get some other parts of the presentation under way? Maybe we could do the boring parts—advertising budget. Stuff like that."

"Sure." She motioned for him to join her at her desk.

He slipped into his chair and leaned forward, resting elbows on her desk. His chin fell into his palms.

God, she was gorgeous.

Polished, sexy, with an air about her. Evidently, he wasn't the only one who'd done some growing up in the past six years. Her taste in clothes, cologne—and hopefully men—had all matured.

Classy. The woman was classy.

He couldn't wait to strip her of all that sophistication and find the gritty, sexy dynamo hiding below the surface. She'd thank him someday. He was sure of it.

Could they possibly take up where they'd left off a little while ago? He scooted his chair closer and leaned a bit, putting his face within inches of hers as he'd done before.

What the heck, it worked once.

"What are you doing?" She smiled.

He donned his most innocent expression—or so he hoped. "What? I'm waiting."

"Waiting for what?" This time, she leaned closer, but didn't touch him. It was sheer torture having her so close. She was chewing gum. He could smell the mint.

"Just waiting for you to get the budget file. What did you think?"

Her mouth was so close her breath dried his lips. Damn it! She was teasing him back...and he loved it! A smile pulled at his mouth.

She jerked back and studied him with keen eyes. "You're full of shit, you walking hard-on."

He laughed. "Guilty as charged, but only with you." Was that another blush he saw coloring her cheeks?

"Liar." A hand lifted, and she palmed her own face before tucking a stray ringlet behind her ear.

He longed to set those glorious curls free—and the woman who possessed them, too. "Are you feeling okay? Still hung over?"

"Yeah. I think that's it."

He didn't believe that for a minute. Nope. She was hot and bothered. Because of him.

A knock sounded at the door, and he turned to see who was there. Fate called out, "Come in."

Duncan stepped into the room.

What the hell was he doing here?

"Good afternoon. How's it going?"

Fate turned pristine white before his eyes. All that sexy pink vanished. "Good, sir."

Duncan nodded and looked to Gabe. "I need to speak with you. In my office. Five minutes."

"Okay." When Duncan left, closing the door behind him, he knew without a doubt what was coming. An ugly knot settled in his gut. "I'll be right back." He stood. Somehow, he had to convince Duncan he needed more time.

"What do you think it is?" She watched him walk to the door, not once letting her gaze stray. She looked worried, and he didn't have the heart to tell her she should be.

"I probably did something stupid and pissed off the brass again. I'll let you know when I get back."

She stood and was next to him in a heartbeat. Her hand settled on his arm. "You'll tell me if it's about me, right? If they want to fire me. I need to know."

"I'll tell you. Promise." What a stupid ass he was! He couldn't tell her that. For one, because he wouldn't let it happen. End of story.

A very pleasing look settled over her face. It was an odd mixture of emotions, but what he thought he saw on the surface was something resembling trust.

He went to Duncan's office, rapped on the door in his usual way, and entered when Duncan called to him behind the closed door.

The VP was sitting behind his desk, and he didn't stand when Gabe entered.

Damn! Duncan was pissed. "Get your ass in here. We need to talk."

"Now, before you get your shorts in a wad—"

"Sit down!" Duncan bellowed.

Gabe sat, noting the bulging veins at the man's temples. This wasn't good.

Duncan slammed his palms on the desk. "What kind of idiot do you think I am, Ryan?"

Was that a rhetorical question? He decided it would be wise to leave that one unanswered.

"This idiotic game must end now! Today! She's gotta go." Duncan stood and walked around the desk, towering over him. "Do you know how many people saw the two of you up there? You made me look like a fool."

"Sorry." Damn it, he knew he should have pulled the shades sooner.

"If you're lucky, the brass hasn't caught wind of it. Yet."

"Well, if they haven't, can't you give her another few days—"

"No!"

Gabe had enough of sitting and being scolded like a preschooler. He stood to his full six feet and relished the extra inches he had over the inflamed VP. "You can't fire her."

"Like hell! I'm the boss, here. Remember?"

"I told you, I'll quit."

"You'd be a fool to do that. You signed a no compete clause, remember? If you quit, you won't get another job."

He shrugged. "Do you really think that matters to me?"

"You're lying."

"Try me." He hadn't been able to hide the challenge in his voice. The man was starting to piss him off, boss or not.

"Damn it, Ryan. What are you trying to do? Get us all fired?"

He couldn't tell Duncan what he was really trying to do. "Um, no. Actually, I'm trying to launch the most kick-ass dating service Detroit has ever seen."

Duncan shook his head. "Well, what have you accomplished so far, besides the obvious?"

He inwardly cringed. Time to dole out some convincing lies. "We've tackled the budget, competition and market analysis."

Duncan looked pleased. He nodded. "Really?"

"Fate and I are a good team. I told you we would be."

"No comment."

"I think you should consider keeping us both—"

"No way in hell."

"Another week?"

Duncan crossed his arms over his chest and eyed him. "No more tonsil hockey in the office. Got it?"

"Yep. Promise."

"Blinds open at all times. I want to see you two working. Busy as bees, or she's outta here."

"Got it."

"I mean it, Ryan. You start pawing her, and she's gone. I don't give a damn about your sad love life. Do what the rest of us do, go to a titty bar on Eight Mile and pay for it."

That gave him an instant case of the shivers. He headed to the door.

"I want the first draft of your report on my desk Monday morning."

"Okay." He didn't take a deep breath until after he shut the door closed behind him.

No kissing. No touching. Open blinds...the man had no heart.

Eight Mile? The man had no life, either.

Sheesh! Clearly the leash had been shortened. That was okay. He'd find a way...a way to help Fate keep her job, and a way into her bed.

Permanently.

But, first, he needed to draft a marketing report. Pronto!

When he returned to Fate's office, he answered her silent inquiry with a smile. "I told you I'd pissed off the brass. I'm such a stupid ass sometimes."

"It had nothing to do with me?"

He gulped. "Nothing." Damn, he hated lying to her! "It had nothing to do with you. They love you."

Her soft smile of relief touched his heart and left him regretting the lie even more. But what the hell else could he do? He was between the proverbial rock and hard place.

In fact, that would not be the last lie he told her, no doubt about it.

He swallowed a boulder of regret and sat back in his chair. "You want to get back to the report? Duncan wants our first draft on his desk by Monday."

"Monday? Oh, my God! We don't have a single section done yet. How will we get it finished in time?"

"Don't worry. We can work together. Between the two of us, we can get it done, even if we have to work all weekend long."

Maybe Duncan had done him a favor… Images of the two of them cozy in his place sent another blaze to his cock. His pants grew instantly snug.

Thank God for demanding bosses!

Chapter Seven
Genius can be a very subjective thing.

Fate's appointment at the dating service took much longer than she expected. She interviewed, posed for pictures, and made a video. Then she scoured the files of dozens of men. It was exhausting.

Yet, she found one. An optometrist. Her age, similar interests. They had a lunch date for tomorrow.

After thanking the very kind, very patient, staff at Let's Do Lunch, she went home and fell right into bed. And of course had nightmares about the date. So much for high hopes. The next morning, she followed her usual routine, and arrived at work ten minutes late, as usual.

Gabe's grin was a welcome sight. "How'd you do last night?" A sight for sore eyes. In fact, he looked damn good today.

"I have a lunch date today, but boy, what an ordeal! It was hard finding the right guy. My age, similar interests. I can't tell you how many videos I watched."

"Yeah, same here. That got me thinking."

She dropped into her chair and checked her message slips. "About what?"

Gabe scooted his chair over to her desk and parked it in its usual spot, close enough to hers for her to smell his aftershave. "Our target market, our niche. I have an idea."

"Let it fly. I'm listening." She leaned back and prepared for some crazy scheme. She almost chuckled as she watched him. He looked so excited, his features danced with enthusiasm. Could he be any sexier?

"I think we should charge them membership fees based on the group they belong to."

What had he said? Somehow his words ended up scrambled by the time they reached her brain. "I'm not following you."

"We could group applicants by age, education, physical appearance."

"I don't know. That sounds a little shallow. Like grading meat."

He shrugged. "That's the way the world works, Fate. Like it or not. Don't you think a gorgeous twenty-something woman would pay a little extra to meet a handsome, successful guy..." He puffed up his chest like a rooster on steroids and winked. "...like myself?"

She laughed. He just loved to exaggerate, and it was damn endearing. "So, carrying this idea a little further. What do we do with the ones that don't fit the mold for prime grade when they want to be a part of it?"

"Don't tell them?"

This idea was just rubbing her the wrong way, and as she watched Gabe toy with a pencil eraser, she wished those fingers were rubbing her...the right way. "Okay, granted, if there had been such a system, I would probably have saved a huge chunk of time last night, but I'm still not sure this whole thing is fair."

"Nothing's fair."

Got that right. She glanced down at her desk. It was useless. Staring at him emptied her mind. How the hell could she carry on a conversation? She rummaged around for the lost thought. *Oh, yeah!* "Let me ask you this, then.

Where do we get all those successful, *busy*, men? Many of them are more apt to avoid our service because they're not in the market for a wife, and second—"

"We offer them free membership."

"What?" *He's an idiot, he's definitely an idiot.* "We can't do that. It's completely unfair to make all the women pay and not the men."

"Well, if they're the ones looking for the service, shouldn't they pay?"

She tried like hell to follow his logic, but it was too twisted. "So are the guys."

"Not really. They'll sign a membership because they don't have anything to lose. The women'll sign because they want something. See? Not the same at all." He smacked his hand down on the desk and stood in triumph. "It's genius! We'll have new members flooding in."

Did she really have to put her name on the marketing report?

"And here I was going to suggest we stick with something safe, like quality customer service."

"We'll have that, too. We'll treat them like kings and queens. They'll love us! We'll be the biggest thing to hit Detroit since the Ford Motor Company."

His enthusiasm was amusing, the way it lit his face and made him hop around like a child at Christmas. She'd like to have him sit on her lap. She'd give him a nice gift..."Don't you think you're going just a little overboard?"

"The brass'll love it! They'll see dollar signs. We'll both get to keep our jobs." He dropped into his chair. "Damn, I'm good."

The cocky smile was just cute enough to make her crotch tingle. "No comment." She hated the idea, wondered if it was fertile ground for lawsuits, but what the heck? She had nothing better. And Monday wasn't all that far away. "What about advertising?"

"We'll look at some demographics. I'd say radio. Drive time."

She shook her head. "Big money there."

"Print advertising in some local papers, edgy papers like Metro Detroit?"

"That's doable. But how will we advertise this? We can't put the groups in our ads if we're going to be selective."

"Yes, selective. Not discriminating. Hmmm. Maybe you're right." He leaned forward and reached across her desk, clearly targeting her legal pad. She wished he was targeting something else. Why was he so damned focused today? "May I?"

She handed it to him, and their fingertips brushed. A zap shot up her arm and down to her crotch. She dropped the pad.

He smiled.

"How the hell do you do that?" She rubbed her fingertips.

"Do what?" The come-hither waggle of eyebrows suggested he knew exactly what she meant.

Well, at least he was flirting a little. She'd begun to think he had lost interest already.

Another jolt shot through her body as she recalled yesterday's events in that very room. She'd been so close to...so ready to... Oh God! She'd wanted him. Plain and simple.

And as she studied the face she'd thought she'd despised for six years, she realized she'd always wanted him. That thought sent her heart into her throat.

Yes, love and hate were very close to the same thing. How did that proverb go?

She spent the rest of the morning wrestling with her body's reaction to his nearness and her mind's insistence on wandering. While he was much more focused on work today, and less apt to tempt her with intentional innuendo and teasing, she still was completely turned on by mid-morning. Her crotch ached for him. Her nerve endings raw, sensitized. Every sensation exaggerated. In a nutshell, she was a mess.

And as the lunch hour neared, she added a whole heap of regret to the mix. For some reason, going on a date with another man just felt wrong. Sure, she wasn't dating Gabe. But, but...she wanted to.

Strike her dead with a lightning bolt! She was ready to revisit Gabe Land.

Gabe gave her a quick slap on the shoulder as she left, and wished her luck on her date. Expecting the opposite, she rehearsed a few dozen excuses to give the guy when she arrived at the restaurant. Why do this? The actual date wouldn't do anything to further their research.

Yeah...hey! What was Gabe up to now?

Feeling like a trap would spring the minute she stepped inside the restaurant, she tensed. Her neck and shoulders became instantly stiff. Great!

She approached the hostess. "Hi, I'm meeting someone. My name's Fate—"

The hostess, a bouncy blonde with a perfect body, interrupted. "This way, please."

Now, that was service. She followed, catching a glimpse of a good looking guy at a nearby table. Blond hair, cut short, tanned skin, athletic. That was him. In the flesh. And just as good looking in person as he was in the video.

Was he a jerk? She almost hoped he was. It would make her hasty escape that much easier.

The hostess stopped at the table and waited for Fate to sit. "Can I get you something to drink?"

Fate looked at the guy, and noted he had a cola. "I'll take a diet."

"Okay. Be right back." The hostess bounced away, saying over her shoulder. "Your waitress will be with you in just a minute."

Fate watched her walk away then turned. Mr. Optometrist wore a pasted on grin that suggested he was as uncomfortable as she was. "I'm sorry. I have no idea what to say. I've never been on a blind date."

"Me, neither. At least we have that much in common. Name's John. John Cameron." He offered his hand. "Good to meet you."

"Fate Doherty." She took his hand in hers, gave it a shake and released it. "This is so weird."

He nodded. "You're my first date through Let's do Lunch."

"Then I guess I can't ask you how you like the service, eh?"

His movements were slow and intentional as he lifted his glass and took a sip. Not once did she note a wandering gaze. Considering the crowd at the restaurant, that was something to respect. "So far, I like it just fine."

"What made you go to a dating service?"

"I'll only answer that question if you will too."

She nodded, and silently thanked the young man who delivered her drink. "Deal."

"I wanted to find someone to spend time with, but I don't go many places where I'd meet women."

"What about your work?"

"The ladies who work with me are all married. And dating patients is a sure road to court."

She nodded. "I can see that."

"What about you?"

"Well, um..." She tried to decide what to tell him. He seemed like a nice enough guy. She couldn't lie. What if he liked her? Wanted a second date? "I'm doing research."

"What kind of research?"

"On dating services. I can't go into detail, because I wouldn't want to get my employer into trouble. Let's just say I'm comparison shopping?"

He smiled and nodded. "Got it. So, guess that means I shouldn't expect a second date, assuming we got along today."

"Probably not."

Those two words seemed to lift a two-ton truck off the man's shoulders. He visibly relaxed and chattered through the entire meal. At the end, she briefly considered accepting a second date and even took his card.

* * * * *

Gabe had never seen rainbow-hued hair before, well, not in a long time. Last he'd seen anyone with Kool-Aid dyed hair was at his buddy's tattoo parlor in downtown Royal Oak. And it had left him speechless.

He didn't have the luxury of being tongue-tied this time.

What he did for love!

He stood and offered his hand, his gaze hopping from one embellishment to another. A silver ring in her eyebrow, a diamond stud in her nose, and a silver ball protruding from her chin. While he wasn't completely immune to the appeal of exotic piercings, this little lady had taken personal adornment to the extreme. "Gabe Ryan. Nice to meet you."

"Starr Crossing." She took his hand and gave it a quick shake before dropping into the chair across from him.

"That's really your name?"

"Check it out." Gum snapping, she flipped open her fuzzy pink backpack and produced a Social Security card. Printed in black and white, Starr Crossing.

He handed her card back across the table. "That's an usual name. I like it."

"I hated it when I was a kid. Don't mind it so much now." She flagged the waitress and ordered a martini then eyed his empty cola glass. "And another one for him too, whatever he's drinking."

"Thanks," he said.

"People tell me I'm too aggressive. I don't see it that way. I just see what needs to be done, and I do it." She tossed her purse aside and slung her arms over the back of her chair. "So, what's your story?"

He dumped an ice cube into his mouth and chewed. "Not much to tell, really."

"Everyone has a story."

"Maybe. But mine's pretty dull."

"You? Dull? For some reason, I highly doubt that." The waiter brought the drinks and Starr thanked him and swallowed her martini in one gulp. Sheesh! He'd never seen a woman who could drink like that. She ordered a second then eyed him with a gaze much too steady for a woman who couldn't weigh more than one hundred pounds, and who'd just downed gin like water. "No, I'm guessing you're a lot like me. You see what you want, and you go for it. You're confident in your masculinity. An animal in bed—"

Heat shot to his face. "Whoa! What makes you say that?"

She pointed at his wrist. "The watch."

"It was a gift from my niece, and I'll wear anything she gives me. The kid has me wrapped around her little finger."

She smiled. "It says *a lot* about you."

"A watch?" He gulped, not at all pleased with her expression. If he had to put a name to it, he'd call it the barracuda-in-a-trout-pond look.

"Are you into tantric sex?"

"Not on a first date." He downed half his cola.

She sighed. "That's too bad. I took off the afternoon, just in case."

"Good planning. Damn!" He slammed his hand on the table, feigning disappointment. "I should have thought to do that. But stupid me, I figured we'd just do lunch, not each other."

"It was worth a shot."

"Sure it was, but I'd hate to see you waste a perfectly good afternoon off. I'm taken, but I've got a couple friends you might like to meet."

"Already pawning me off, eh?" She picked up her menu and waved it at the waitress. "We haven't even ordered yet."

"I'm not pawning. That's not what I'm trying to do."

"Then what are you trying to do?"

"Truth?"

She nodded. "Nothing but."

"I'm trying to convince the woman I love that I'm the best guy for her."

Her eyebrows scrunched together. "By going on a date with me? I'm not following you."

"Are you in the mood to listen to a long story?"

"Sure! What the hell. I took the afternoon off. Amuse me."

"Have you ever loved someone so much you'd do anything to get them to notice you? Even be obnoxious, make a fool out of yourself, risk your career. Just to catch a glimpse of a smile?"

Starr shook her head. "She must be something special."

"Fate is. I've known her for years, since college. We dated for a short time, but we were young, and I was stupid. My mother died when I was young, and my father wasn't exactly the best role model for how to treat a woman." He closed his eyes and let images from his college days wash through his mind. "I still remember the first time I saw her. She slipped on the ice outside the cafeteria, and I helped her up. She was so beautiful, so smart. After the first touch, I was hooked. I didn't want to let her go for nothing. My roommates teased me to no end. Said I was whipped. And I admit it, I fell. Hard. I even let my grades go and almost lost my scholarship. All that mattered was being with her."

"That's very romantic. So what happened?" Starr took a forkful of salad into her mouth and chewed.

"She decided to move on, not that I could blame her. I wasn't mature enough. My father was so determined to make up for our not having a mother, he babied the hell out of both me and my older brother. It took years for me to grow up, but since then, I've been trying to break through her resistance. Hell, I'd even provoke her because it was better than indifference. And it's worked." He smiled. "It's finally worked."

* * * * *

When Fate returned to the office, she caught the look on Gabe's face. It was an odd expression, one of expectation and maybe a hint of a few other things. Impossible to read.

"Well?" he asked, scooting his chair back to its position at the side of her desk. She wondered why he even bothered to move it to his desk. It didn't stay there long.

"Well, it was okay."

"Just okay?" His eyebrows raised behind a cascade of runaway curls on his forehead. She was tempted to toy with them. They looked so silky. Soft.

"The guy was nice enough. Smart. Good looking. A little funny…" What had been missing? That spark? That irresistible urge to get close? The immediate rush of tingly expectation between her legs, The Gabe Factor. "What about you?"

"I had a good time. She was very…" He raised his gaze to the ceiling. "Very colorful. Smart. Creative. Unique."

"Sounds like she was right up your alley. Did she like your watch?"

"She didn't comment on it."

"Was she attractive?"

"In an urbane way, I suppose."

What did that mean? "Would you go out with her again?"

He shrugged.

Was he trying to make her jealous? A spike of something shot up her spine.

By God, she was jealous!

"So," she said, trying like hell to swallow the ugly feeling in her gut, "what did we learn from this exercise?"

"That you missed me?"

She didn't like that answer. "No, remember, we did this for research?"

He grinned. "Oh, yeah. What's wrong?" He leaned a little closer…too close…no, not close enough…

Oh, hell! He was doing it again! Her whole body tingled. Her nerve endings ignited.

She thought about reaching for him and kissing that cocky grin off his lips. "Nothing's wrong. What makes you ask a question like that?"

He shrugged. "You just look a little tense." He glanced at the window then moved away.

She took a deep breath. Why did he move? Had she said something wrong? "I could say the same thing about you."

He slumped back in his chair. "I'd say I learned we have some tough competition in the market and need to have a very specific strategy if we're going to survive."

"Well, did we really have to go through all the trouble of a blind date to figure that out?"

Pencil in hand, he reached forward, running the eraser up her jaw line. "Maybe not. But I thought it might be fun."

"Well..." What was she going to say? Those shocking gray eyes were hypnotizing her, wiping her brain clean. She couldn't put a coherent thought together.

"What?"

"Um..." Out of sheer desperation, she dropped her gaze. Much better! At least she could think. "Next time you think something might be amusing, maybe you should leave me out."

"Never. Besides, I don't think you'd appreciate that one bit."

A fingertip tickled her neck, just below her ear. Her head, of its own accord tipped, giving him full access to the sensitive skin. Her mind went blank again.

"I thought you had a nice lunch," he said, his voice so incredibly seductive, she'd swear she could come right there.

"I did. He even wanted to go out on a second date." Why had she told him that? Did she really want him to know? Did she want him to be jealous?

Would he be?

"Really," he drawled. His fingertips trailed higher, and he tugged at the scrunchy at her nape. Her curls spilled over her shoulders, and he gripped them and tugged. Not too hard. Just hard enough. Damn!

Her panties became instantly wet.

She smiled. Wouldn't he like to see those panties! Red lace. A thong. They made her feel just a little naughty, and she wondered what he would say, how he would look, if she lifted her skirt.

"You like that?" he whispered.

"Yeah."

"You want to get outta here? Go somewhere private to talk?"

Now, things were going the right direction! She met his gaze. "Do you honestly want to talk?"

He tugged again. "What do you think?"

As if her thong wasn't soaked enough!

* * * * *

His cock was ready, so hard he could penetrate marble.

He needed to get the hell out of the office. Now. He took Fate's hand. Where to go?

His place was too far. "Can we go to your place?"

Fate nodded but didn't say a word. She simply followed him. She looked as flush-faced as he'd ever seen her, and if he was a betting man, he'd put money on the fact that she was as ready to fuck as he was. For appearances sake, he released Fate's hand long before they reached the bottom of the staircase.

He stopped at the reception desk and told Alexa they were going to check out another competitor. Alexa gave him a knowing smile.

That woman knew him too well.

Then again, that was his fault. Their brief relationship—if you'd call it that—a couple years ago had been a big mistake. It hadn't worked from day one, but it had taken Alexa almost a full year to accept it.

If he didn't know better, he'd swear the woman was attempting a silent plea. Knowing her, she wanted a threesome.

He didn't wait around to find out if that was where she was headed. Instead, he dropped behind Fate and settled a hand on the base of her spine, just above that hot ass.

Damn, he loved the way it swayed when she walked.

If he didn't possess a fair amount of control, he'd have come right there.

"Whose car should we take?" Fate asked over her shoulder.

"We can take mine."

"What if we don't make it back?"

"We'll either pick it up later, or I can drive you to work tomorrow morning."

"Okay."

He unlocked the door for her and caught a glimpse of delectable cleavage as she dropped into the seat. She looked up at him, a sexy smile curving two perfect lips. Then she released one more button.

"Tease," he grumbled. Her giggles greeted him as he took the driver's seat and started the car. In a heartbeat, they were on their way.

Her hand slid between his legs, and he almost went blind with need.

"Mmmm..." she whispered. "Someone's hard."

He blew out a huff of air. "That's an understatement."

"I can't wait to run my tongue from the base of that cock to the tip."

His hard-on strained against his pants. He tried like hell to pay attention to what he was doing, or he knew he'd end up parking the car in the middle of a tree.

A wicked smile on her face, she unzipped his khakis. "Damn! You're huge. I don't remember you being that big." She squeezed at the base then slowly pulled up. Before he could stop her, she leaned down and teased the head with her tongue.

White heat shot through his body. His eyelids grew so heavy he needed tent stakes to keep them up. His cock reared against his stomach.

He pulled into a parking lot at the back of a wooded park. Good thing school didn't let out for an hour or so. He turned off the car, yanked up his pants, and went around to the passenger side. She watched him, visibly curious.

He'd never fucked in his car. It was tiny, cramped. But what the hell? He opened the passenger door and hit the passenger side seat recline lever. "I can't wait another minute."

"I like the sound of that."

He took another glance around. Not a soul. Then he reached between her legs. "I want to taste you."

She turned in her seat, facing him, and leaned down to remove her shoes. Then she stood and shimmied out of her pantyhose. "This is intense—in a park. I've never done it outside before. Kind of dangerous."

Good God! The motion she used to wiggle out of those pantyhose was driving him nuts. "Does that make you hot?"

She nodded and sat, hiking her skirt up around her hips.

His gaze fixed on one spot. Between her legs. What was she wearing? Red? "Stand up."

She stood.

"Turn around and lift your skirt."

She did as he asked, flashing him the roundest, hottest ass he'd ever seen. Another burst of heat shot to his cock. "Bend over the hood."

She did, glancing over her shoulder, a playful smile on her face. Damn it! Where did she learn to do that? She was driving him crazy with that look.

He slid a finger inside her. She was so wet. He could take her right there. Her legs quivered as he thrust two fingers inside. "Do you like that?"

"Ohhh...yeah..."

"Get back in the car."

She settled in her seat, her legs spread wide for him. He pulled the wet thong aside and parted her thatch of red hair. When he licked her clit she moaned, her tight abs clenching. She tasted sweet, absolutely intoxicating. He needed more.

He lifted her knees and spread them wider, then plunged two fingers inside as he laved her folds. Her hips gyrated in tempo to his hand as he plunged in and out.

She tasted so good. Smelled so good. Felt so good.

He had to fuck her.

He pulled her legs until her ass was on the edge of the seat then kneeled, and in one smooth stroke he was inside.

Fuck! She was tight. Hot. Ready. He felt his come at the base of his cock. Could he hold back? He quit moving.

And then she squeezed that tight cunt, clamping around him. It was all he could do to keep himself from filling her.

He thumbed her clit and she moaned again, parting her legs further. "Oh, yeah." He felt the telling pulse around his cock as she came. Her back arched, and he hammered her until he reached his own orgasm.

His breathing came in short bursts as he opened his eyes.

She smiled up at him. "Fuck me again."

His cock, which had begun to slacken inside her, hardened readily.

He regretfully pulled out and pulled up his drawers. "Let's get to your place first. I want more room next time. I want access to every inch of you."

Her eyes sparkled. "I can't wait." She closed her legs—a crime—and turned to face forward.

He zipped his pants and sat in the driver's seat. In ten torturous minutes they parked in her driveway. She gathered her hose and shoes from the back seat as he came around to open her door.

She led him into the house and dropped her belongings on a table by the front door. When he stepped inside, she shut the door behind him. "Something to drink?"

"Sure. I'd love a glass of ice water."

"Okay." She didn't walk to the kitchen.

What was she doing?

She lifted her hands, releasing each button of her blouse slowly, letting him drink in the sight of her chest as it was slowly revealed. When she shrugged out of her blouse, letting it slip to the floor, he lunged at her. She stepped back. "Uh uh! You had your fun. Now it's my turn."

She reached between her breasts and unhooked her bra—a front loader. Cool. When she opened it, two perfect breasts with pink nipples stood erect.

He wanted to touch her. He needed to touch her.

She shook her head as though she'd read his mind. "Not yet."

Then she reached down and unhooked her skirt, shimmying out of it. There was that hip action thing again. It was driving him crazy.

She had great legs. Tight stomach. Hips with just enough curve. She turned around.

And a perfect ass.

The sight of that red thong running up the center left him burning.

She bent over and ran her hand over her ass.

Damn! Fuck! His cock strained against his pants.

Turning, she smiled. "Do you like what you see?"

"Oh baby. You're perfect."

She smiled. "Take off your clothes. I want to see you."

He didn't need a written invitation. Off came the shirt, pants, shoes, socks and shorts. His cock reared up against his stomach as he stood before her, relishing the way her gaze traveled over his body.

She sighed. "You have the most amazing body I've ever seen. What do you do? Spend hours in the gym every day?"

"Maybe one."

She nodded. "Whatever you're doing, it's working. I'm wet just looking at you."

"Can I touch you yet?" All he could think about was getting back inside that tight cunt.

With a tip of her head, she gave him her answer. And in two quick strides he was on her, his mouth devouring hers. His hands teasing two nipples then slipping down to cup that ass.

Someday he'd fuck it, if she let him.

She ground her hips into him, rubbing those slick folds up and down his cock as he dropped to the floor. She forced him onto his back.

God! That was a sight. Her on top. That face, those tits. Her stomach.

She straddled him then dropped a hand, a fingertip rubbing her clit. Her head dropped back, and he watched, mesmerized by the sight of her masturbating over him.

Inch by inch, she lowered herself down, taking him deep. Her slick pussy walls welcomed him inside, at first opening to accommodate his girth, then clamping tight.

His own moan shot from his chest. She lifted her hips and slammed down again, and he cried out. He couldn't stand it. He had to take control.

"What's wrong?" she asked, her voice teasing.

"Not a damn thing. That's the problem."

She shot him a wicked grin then spun around, his cock still deep inside. Now he had a full view of her back and ass as she rode him. That ass slapped the base of his stomach, and he felt the flood of come shoot up his cock.

And then the pulsing of her pussy.

They cried out in unison as they came together, both their bodies wracked by throbbing, pulsing, mind-numbing heat.

And when it was over, she stood and pulled him up, leading him to the bedroom. They lay in bed, his arms wrapped around that amazing body, his eyelids heavy, his mind awash in that muddy after sex bog.

He would never forget today, the day his precious Fate had finally returned to him. I should do a list. White picket fence, La-Z-boys, big TV and a dog.

"Do you think we should go back to work?" she asked.

"Nope."

"Do you want something to eat?"

"Nope."

"Drink?"

"Nope. All I want is you. Here. In my arms."

She sighed and snuggled closer, her head in the crook of his arm.

Yes, this is exactly what he'd wanted all these years. Fate Doherty was finally his.

Chapter Eight
Getting what you want always comes at a price.

Fate couldn't remember ever feeling so at ease with another human being. Normally after sex, a dark, gloomy mood fell over her. Not this time. She wondered why.

It felt so right having him there with her, in her home, in her bed, snuggled so close. Her head rested on his chest, rising and falling with each breath he took. His heartbeat thumped in her ear.

"Tell me about your life since college. Outside of the obvious, what's happened between now and then?" she asked, relishing the feel of his hand running up and down her arm.

"Well, I've been working, but you know that already."

"Did you ever marry?"

"Nope."

She lifted her head and looked at him. "Why not?"

"What about you?"

"Aren't you going to answer my question first?"

"No. You first." He smiled.

"I didn't get married." She sat up, fluffed a couple pillows and leaned back against them. "Never found the right one."

He rolled over on his side, propped himself up on an elbow, and rested his head in his hand. His bicep swelled. Yum. "Who's the right one?"

"I don't know." *You?* "I've just been waiting for that feeling, that certainty you see in the movies. Do you think it's real?"

"Yep. I know it is."

Her gaze wandered over his face, and a knot tightened in her gut. "You sound so sure."

"I am."

She didn't have to ask what he was talking about. It was all over his face.

Was he the right one for her? Was there any doubt? Funny, in less than a week, she'd gone from hating the man to…to falling in love with him? Could it be? How had that happened?

Unless she'd never stopped loving him. There was that love-hate thing again.

"Do you want to be married?" He wound a finger in her hair.

"I've always dreamed of being married, having kids. A part of me wants to jump off the fast track and enjoy raising a couple of babies, stay at home, maybe even home school."

His eyebrows rose to impossible heights. "Really?"

"Is it that hard to believe? Fate Doherty— independent, career focused—wants to stay at home and have babies."

"A little. But, it's a nice surprise. What about your husband? What're you looking for?"

Someone like you…no, not like you. Just you. "I don't really have a laundry list. Just a vague notion. Um, a man who is caring, committed, hard-working but able to balance his career with family time. Funny and smart.

Shares interests with me but also has some of his own. A man I can grow old with but never tire of."

He chuckled. "And you said you don't have a laundry list?"

She enjoyed the sound of that laughter, and imagined enjoying it for decades. "What about you?"

"Sexy, sexy, and sexy."

She gave him a jab in the belly, and he laughed. "Seriously."

He sat up, and crossed his arms behind his head, making his chest look incredibly wide. "Well, I am a guy. We men do like that sort of thing."

"Okay, Mr. Deep," she teased.

He laughed and dropped an arm. His hand wrapped around hers and he gave it a squeeze, and a warm tingle spread through her chest. "I want a wife who is intelligent, funny, charming, attractive, loving, devoted...I want you."

Oh God! Her eyes burned. She wanted to believe those words. She'd never heard them before. At least, not from someone she'd actually consider taking seriously. She pulled her hand free and gave him another playful tap. "You're just saying that so we can have more sex." Her pussy tingled.

He shrugged. "I'd take more sex if it's offered. But I'm serious. Why don't you believe me?"

"Because you're a dog. Everyone knows that."

"You're going to believe rumors over me?" He almost looked insulted, except for the twinkle in his eye.

"Maybe." Despite the heat rising to her face, she tried to appear indifferent. She crossed her arms over her chest.

"What happened between you and that receptionist…what's her name? Alena?"

"Alexa. We dated for a short time a couple of years ago. But it didn't work out."

She wasn't sure she wanted to know more, but she couldn't resist asking, "Why?"

"She's a little…wild."

This was getting interesting. She turned to face him. "Wild? Isn't that what guys like?"

"I'm not into swinging. She is. The sex parties, partner swapping, guy-on-guy, girl-on-girl, the whole ball of wax. That isn't my scene. Plain and simple."

"Oh." *Whew! Big sigh of relief!* "So, what happened in your last relationship? Why did it fail?"

"Alexa was the last woman I dated."

"Two years ago?"

"I told you, I know what I want. I'm not the Don Juan everyone makes me out to be. I think they just assume I'm running around sleeping with anything in a skirt because I'm so quiet about my private life."

She wanted to believe him, but what if he was giving her a line of shit? It could all be a lie…couldn't it? How could she possibly learn the truth?

Did it matter? So what if he'd been a player? That was before. People changed when they settled down. She'd seen that with friends. Young women who'd been as wild as any guy in their twenties turned into regular Suzy Homemakers when they married. It happened.

He stretched his arms overhead, biceps flexing, shoulder muscles bunching. That was one hell of a nice body.

And maybe, someday, it could be hers to enjoy for the rest of her life. Maybe those silver-gray eyes, years from now ringed with deep creases, would look at her with love. Maybe endearing words of affection and commitment would come from those perfect lips. And maybe they'd share those silent moments of contentment, sitting in the shade and watching their grandchildren play in the yard.

Wow! Had her dreams changed. Or had those wishes always been there, tucked below the surface? Had she just avoided them because she'd feared they'd never come to be?

Maybe that hatred had been displaced pain.

Oh, she was done trying to figure herself out! She liked the way things were going. Why mess it up by overanalyzing it?

Yes, about the only thing she should be doing at the moment was enjoying the body lying beside her. She reached over and ran a fingertip down the center of his chest. His stomach muscles tensed, making them even more pronounced. Yummy. She glanced lower.

His stomach muscles weren't the only things more pronounced. Unable to resist, she gripped his hard-on in her hand and squeezed.

He drew in a deep breath through his nose and growled. "You, my dear, are insatiable. I love it." He pushed her flat on her back, pinning her by the shoulders.

She stared up into that sexy, flushed face of his, heated by the hunger in his eyes, and wrapped her legs around his waist. "So what do you think about going another round?"

"I'd say you're on. But I need something first."

"Oh?" She liked the glitter in his eyes. It made promises that sent throbbing waves to her pussy. "What do you need?"

"Got any KY jelly?"

"Sure. In the nightstand."

He released her shoulders, but remained straddled over her hips as he leaned over and retrieved the tube from the drawer. She, being hotter than she'd ever been, took his dick in her hand and slowly slid up and down the length. He was huge, bigger than anyone she'd had before. That glorious cock was the picture of perfection. In every sense of the word.

Tube of lubricant in hand, he grinned, crawled off her, and rumbled, "Roll over."

What was he going to do? Curious, she complied.

"You have the world's most perfect ass." He drew her legs apart, wide apart, knees bent, inner thigh muscles stretched.

That was an incredibly sexy feeling, so exposed.

He kneaded her ass cheeks then separated them. As if she hadn't felt exposed before! Her pussy throbbed, ready and eager for that giant cock of his. Her nerve endings from hair roots to toes lit aflame.

And when she felt the first touch of his tongue to her tight hole, she just about bucked him off. No one had ever eaten her there!

She felt a fingertip, slick and warm, slide up and down her crack. Oh, the ecstasy of that exploring touch. It slid into her pussy, and she clamped her muscles around it, willing it to never leave.

But it did, this time teasing her asshole.

She relaxed, knowing what was to come.

And he didn't disappoint her. His slender finger slowly delved deeper and deeper, the slight pinch of pain nothing compared to the surge of pleasure rippling through her body. Her pussy screamed to be filled, getting so wet she felt the juices flowing outside. She tipped her ass up, willing him to go deeper.

He slid his finger out. "Damn, that ass is perfect. I want to fuck it so very, very badly. Will you let me? I promise I will make it *extremely* good for you."

A shiver of fear shot up her spine. Sure, she knew about anal sex, but she had never done it. She'd watched a few movies, saw how excited men got when they had sex *this* way. But it had to hurt, didn't it? Hurt like hell, she figured. "I don't know." Yet, as he continued stroking and teasing, a part of her shrieked its approval, sending another wave of wetness to her pussy. There was something so arousing, so naughty, about the image of him 'fucking her ass'.

"Scout's honor. I'll go slow, and if you want me to stop at any moment, I will." He teased her ass with the tip of his penis, while his fingers performed magic on her clit.

"You were a boy scout? I never would have guessed." She raised herself on hands and knees.

Still teasing her ass, he pushed two fingers into her pussy. "You should see my Family Life badge."

"Oh…" She sighed. His touches and strokes were driving her insane. "And if they'd had one for lovemaking, I'm sure you'd have one of those, too."

"Do you trust me? Let me show you how wonderful it can be." He softly stroked her ass.

Yes, she wanted it. With him, she did. Her pussy muscles twitched. A flood of heat seeped over her whole body. "Okay."

He parted her ass cheeks with his hands and ran the tip of his cock up and down, teasing her labia, slick and hot, and her pussy. He drove deep into her, and she screamed. Damn, he filled her completely. She clamped her muscles closed around him, and he moaned, leaning low over her back.

And then, with his cock still deep inside, he slowly worked two slick fingers inside her anus, stretching it, sliding in slowly then out in time with his cock. It was almost more than she could take. Her mind was lost to her, adrift somewhere in a frenzied sea of sensations. Of smells and sounds and feelings.

Her pussy clenched around his cock, her ass tightened around his fingers, and she nearly wept from the joy of it.

And then, just as she felt herself nearing completion, he pulled out.

"Hey!" Her body thrummed with the need to leap over the pinnacle. She reached between her legs and found her clit, stroking it lightly with her own fingertip.

"Oh yes, baby, touch yourself." He parted her ass cheeks again, and her stomach muscles clenched in expectation.

Slowly, he pushed his erection inside her tight ass, a tiny fraction of an inch at a time. He murmured in her ear, "Sweetie, relax for me. Let me make it good for you."

It burned, but as he went deeper and deeper, the bite lessened and the pleasure heightened. She opened herself to him, and he drove in entirely, his hips pushing against her buttocks. "Oh."

"That's it. Now touch yourself."

She drew tight circles over her clit with a finger as he slowly slid his cock out and in again. On fire, she quickened the pace. She was close, and it was wonderful. Her entire body stiffened. "Oh...My..."

And then it soared.

Her pussy spasms left her breathless and begging for more. Her ass milked his cock, the muscles spasming in time with her pussy. She rode the climax, willing it to last forever, and it damn near did. And then she felt him swell even more as he reached his own climax and filled her ass with his hot come.

He howled, bucked and pumped his seed inside, and then dropped on trembling arms, his chest and stomach pressed against her back, his cock still buried deep in her ass. "My God, what you do to me." He kissed her neck and shoulders. "Are you okay?"

What had he asked? She was lost in a fog, a wonderful fog. "Mmmm."

"I take it that means yes?" He slid out, and her asshole quivered.

Feeling completely stoned, she rolled on her back and smiled. "That was incredible." Her eyelids drifted closed and she felt herself dozing.

"What do you think?" He kissed her nose and closed eyelids.

"I think..." *Correction—I know.* "I'm thinking I might be falling—"

A cell phone rang. Somewhere in the living room.

"Damn it!" Gabe jumped up, leaving her lying on the rumpled bed alone.

Bewildered and disappointed, she looked up. "What is it?"

He dashed out, and she listened to his distant voice. When he didn't return in a moment, she donned her robe and went to find him.

He ended the call as she entered the room. "I have to leave."

"What's wrong?"

"Damn it! I'm sorry. I can't tell you. Not now. I've got to go, but I'll call you later, okay?" He bent over and found his underwear, then his pants. Those on, he slid his arms into his wrinkled shirt and slipped on his socks and shoes.

"But what about my car?"

"I'll call you later."

"But—" She stopped herself. Whatever the emergency was, it had to be important. He was rushing around like a man who'd been caught by his wife... No way! She wouldn't finish that thought. "Is it work?" she asked.

He gave her a quick hug and a peck on the lips then headed for the door. "I know this looks bad, but please trust me. I have to go. Now."

A chill slid up her spine. She hugged herself. "Okay."

And then he was gone.

What was going on?

Chapter Nine
*Sometimes the least likely prospect
makes the most sense.*

"Ryan, what the hell are you trying to do to me?" Duncan stood cross-armed, cross-legged, cross-every-thing.

"Nothing at the moment. Why?"

He charged at Gabe like a pissed off rhino as soon as the office door was shut. "You may be the best marketing guy in town, but that won't stop me from firing you, especially if I have to choose between your ass and mine." He slammed his fist against the door behind Gabe's head.

"Do what you have to, but please, don't fire Fate."

"I'm going to fire both your asses. What kind of idiot do you take me for? I told you to knock off this ridiculous chase and do your job."

"I did."

"Bullshit! Get your act together, Ryan. No pussy is worth your career."

"This one is."

"Damn it!" He slugged the door again. "How am I going to get this through your thick skull? I'm done with this game. Got it? Do your job. She's done, as of today."

"No, please." He'd pushed too hard. Duncan had no reason to play along. "I know I've taken advantage of our friendship, and I shouldn't have. But, I'm begging you. Don't fire her now. She's trying to get a mortgage. She needs the job. Fire me. You know she'll do the work, won't be distracted if I'm gone."

"You're the best—correction, you were the best."

"Not if I'm not doing the job."

Duncan scrubbed his face with his palms. "You're putting me in a real shitty position here, Ryan. I don't like this package deal you're offering."

"She needs some time. That's all I'm asking for. I don't care how you do it. Demote me. I'll work for her."

"That's stupid."

"But it'll get the brass off your back, right?"

"Not entirely. Alexa went over my head, thanks to her personal...affiliations...with Bradford. She told them you admitted your trip out of the office was for personal reasons."

"Bitch! I never said that. I told her we were checking out the competition. I don't know where she got that other idea."

"You have anything to prove she's lying?"

"No."

"Now you see where I'm at." Duncan walked around his desk and sat. "Come up with something, by tomorrow morning, or both you and Doherty will be standing in the unemployment line. You have to see I'm being more than fair about this. But I'm done being jerked around. I have three ex-wives to support and a car payment to make. I can't be out of a job. Damn lawyers'll be knocking down my door in a week."

"Okay. I'm sorry. I never meant to put your job at risk. I'll give you a report tomorrow, and I'll buckle down. The old Gabe Ryan will be in the office tomorrow."

"That's what I want to hear! Now, about Doherty—"

"Don't fire her. Not yet. She needs this job. I'll help her."

"I can't keep her. I'll demote her."

"Not yet. Give her another week." He rested his hands on Duncan's desk and looked him in the eye. "Please."

"What is with you and that woman anyway? She's cute all right, but why would you throw your career away for her? What's so special about her?"

"What isn't special about her? This is the woman I've loved for years. Have you ever been in love with a goddess? Someone you can't believe would ever love you back? She's a perfect diamond, and I'm clay. For years I didn't know how to talk or act around her. I knew what she saw when she looked at me. How could I change that? How could she learn to love clay?"

"I've never seen you act like this."

"She's the one."

"There's no such thing. I've been married three times. If anyone would know, it'd be me. She'll change, you know that don't you? The minute you put a rock on her finger, she'll blow up like a balloon and turn into a cold bitch that won't spread her legs without a crowbar."

"Not Fate. I know she won't."

"You're an idiot." Duncan shook his head. "I never thought you were so stupid."

"Stupid, happy, what's the difference?" Gabe opened the door. "Like I said, I'll have that report on your desk tomorrow. And I promise to come through. Thanks!" He left before Duncan had a chance to reconsider.

Whew! He'd nearly lost that battle.

In fact, he couldn't call it much of a victory. He'd maybe bought a few days, if he could keep his end of the bargain.

And how the hell would he keep his mind on work with Fate Doherty in the same room? Shit! It was his turn to rub his face with his palms. How? All she had to do was sit there, silent, and she'd be a distraction.

He glanced around the front office, a collection of cubicles running in rows up and down the open space. The telemarketers used those. Cramped, with only a phone and a cheat sheet pinned to the wall, they were a miserable place to work.

Perfect.

Grateful the telemarketers had been laid off for the next two weeks, he found one in the back corner. And as he left the office, he prepared the speech he'd give Fate. He couldn't tell her too much, or she'd think he was still the immature, manipulative child he was years ago...and probably was to this day.

After all, he was not just risking his career anymore. He was also putting Duncan's and Fate's at risk too.

There was no option. He had to make it work.

* * * * *

Fate looked at the clock again. Almost eight.

He didn't call last night. He hadn't called yet this morning. How would she get to work?

What was going on?

She lifted the phone and flopped open the phone book. It would have to be a cab. She didn't dare wait to see if he would show up.

After placing the order, she hung up, gathered her things, and sat on the couch.

Something was very wrong. That familiar dark mood settled over her. It matched the ugly weather outside, gray, chilly.

But then his car pulled into her driveway, and her heart jumped. He'd come. He hadn't forgotten. Would he explain last night to her?

She didn't wait for him to knock. Instead, she cancelled the cab and dashed outside. He opened the passenger side door and she sat, waiting until he was in the driver's seat before speaking, "I wasn't sure you were coming."

"I had some important things to deal with last night." He shifted the car into reverse and backed out of the driveway. "I'm sorry I didn't call." He looked at her as he shifted into drive. "I know I said I would, and you have every right to be pissed."

Donning her "everything's good" mask, even though her stomach weighed at least a ton, she smiled. "I'm not *pissed*. But I'd like to know what's going on. Can you tell me?"

"Alexa got us into some trouble yesterday, filling Bradford's head with a bunch of bullshit. I had to straighten it out."

"Oh, no." She saw the pink slip coming… They were going to fire both her and Gabe. Her heavy-as-lead stomach flamed. "Why would she do that?"

"Because she's a bitch." He glanced at her then reached out and squeezed her shoulder. "I have the situation under control. I wrote up a report to prove she's lying. But I have to move my office. I can't work with you anymore."

"Why?" She couldn't believe it. She was going to miss him. Her office would be so empty.

"Again, to prove she's lying. We'll work over the phone. I'll be in a cubicle out front."

"Okay." She nodded, hoping she appeared outwardly agreeable. Inside, she was in turmoil. She believed him, sort of. There was that nagging doubt. Why would Alexa do such a spiteful thing? She had to have a reason.

Jealousy? That made sense. Although two years was a long time to cling to a dead relationship...unless it hadn't been two years ago.

"Anyway. We'll probably get a lot more done this way. You know I can't concentrate when I'm near you." He glanced at her, his gaze hot.

She swallowed. "It is hard."

"That's the truth." He smiled. "We have to get half of the rough draft of our report done by today if we're going to have any hope of turning in a reasonably complete project on Monday."

"Is Duncan going to fire me then?"

"No." He looked her in the eye. "Trust me. He won't."

Her face warmed, and she dropped her gaze. "I just get the feeling I'm on borrowed time, like he can't wait to show me the door."

"Not at all." He drove into the parking lot and shut off the car. "Now, let's go get that report done and prove what geniuses we are."

She didn't wait for him to open her door. But she did accept a hand out. She didn't miss the way he stiffened as they walked into the building and passed Alexa's desk.

Alexa gave them both a smile. "Good morning."

"Good morning." Fate climbed the stairs and shot Gabe a look before parting ways.

With a tip of the head, he encouraged her on. "I'll call you."

"Okay." She flipped on her lights, took a seat, read through her mail and messages, and skimmed the packet Michael had left on her desk.

It was too damn quiet.

The phone rang, and she snapped it up. "Gabe?"

"Hello, Ms. Doherty? This is Ms. Meyers from the bank. I'm sorry for calling you at work."

"It's okay. What's up?" She held her breath, not sure if the phone call meant good news or bad.

"We have a problem."

Bad! Oh no. Her heart sunk to her toes, not that it had far to go anyway. After Gabe's news it was already down somewhere around her knees. "What's wrong?"

"I'm reading the appraisal. It just came in. It's much too low."

"How much?" She grabbed her doodle pad and started scribbling with a pencil.

"About twenty thousand."

"Oh." Damn! Where would she get that kind of cash?

"You can get one-oh-five, unless you want to find another house. You've been pre-approved for one-thirty."

"Okay. I'll have to think about this. Figure out what I can do."

"All right, then. I'll wait to hear back."

"Thank you." She hung up the phone. "Damn it!" She needed some sanity. There was only one place she would find that. She punched Tracy's number.

* * * * *

"So, what's the big emergency this time?" Tracy, looking her cool, corporate self, sat at the table, stirring a cola with a straw.

Fate sat, ordered a diet from the hostess, and rested her elbows on the table. She dropped her chin into her palms. "My life is a mess."

"That bad?" Tracy smiled.

"I'm serious this time."

"So, what's going on? You aren't going to make me pry it out of you, are you?"

The waitress brought Fate's drink, took her order, and left. Fate took a long swig. The cool liquid felt good going down.

"Well, let's see. I think I've fallen in love with Gabe—"

Tracy slammed her hand on the table. "I knew it! See? What did I tell you."

"Yeah, yeah."

"So, what's wrong with that?"

"I don't know. He's amazing. And I won't tell you how *oh-my-God-how-incredible* he is in bed." A smile tugged at her lips and heat shot to her groin and face simultaneously. "But something's up. He's acting weird."

Tracy cocked her head. "Weird? How?"

"Well, we were doing great, granted getting carried away at work. Then we slept together, and he got a phone call, ran out of my house, and now he won't stay in the same room with me."

Tracy scowled. "That doesn't sound good. Has he explained why?"

"He claims an ex-girlfriend from two years ago got us into trouble with the powers-that-be, and he doesn't want to give her any more ammunition."

"Do you believe him?"

"I do...I think. I mean, she doesn't act like a scorned woman." She took another drink. "So, I have that to contend with, plus I have the feeling they're going to fire me any day. Gabe says they aren't, but I don't think I believe him. Plus, I got a call about the house."

"Yeah?" Tracy glanced over her shoulder. The waitress set their salads down, Tracy poked distractedly at a tomato.

"The appraisal's too low. Twenty thousand too low."

"What're you going to do?"

"I have no idea. You're the numbers person. You tell me."

Tracy chewed, eyeing the ceiling. "What about your sister, Destiny? Can she help?"

"Nope. She's 'horny-mooning' somewhere in Europe. Brian wanted to see the world. It's kind of strange, if you ask me. He kept saying that finally he was free. No, I'd hate to ruin this for them. Besides, after the wedding and this trip, I doubt they have two nickels to rub together.

"Oookaay, you could take out a loan against your 401K. It's tax-free money. They'll take it out of your paycheck."

"I hadn't thought of that." A little bit of weight lifted from her shoulders. "Thanks." She took a bite of her salad. Creamy. Yum. "Wonder how much twenty-thousand will cost me a week."

"It'll be a chunk." Tracy lifted her eyes and blinked, a common thing for Tracy to do when she was calculating. "Almost four hundred a week if you want to pay it back in a year. Of course, there's another problem."

Four hundred! "Oh? As if the first one wasn't enough to make me run for the hills?"

"If Gabe's wrong, and you're fired, the loan is due within thirty days, or you have to pay taxes and penalties on the money."

"Oh..." The weight just returned to her shoulders. Full force. "Thirty days? What would I pay in taxes and penalties?"

"Um...about five thousand?"

"Hell!"

"Sorry." Tracy shook her head. "Maybe you should just give up? Buy something else."

"I can't give up. My mother wants to live in her own house. I can't let her down. Shit!"

"I wish I had the money—I mean, I do, but it's tied up right now. I'd loan it to you if I could."

"No, that's okay. I wouldn't take a loan from you, anyway. You know that." She swallowed a sigh and some more salad. "I just have to come up with another idea."

She glanced at her watch. "Better get back to work while I still have a job."

"Sorry I couldn't be more help."

"You were. Just listening to me rave is a help. Gets it out of my system." She flagged the waitress and asked for a box and the check.

The waitress nodded, handed her the check and then ran off to get a box. Disappointed that Tracy hadn't handed her an easy solution to her problem like she'd hoped, Fate gave Tracy her share of the tab and tip, thanked her again, and returned to work. Still no better off than she had been when she'd left.

This just plain sucked.

Was there a way?

She half-ran to her office.

"You're in a mighty big hurry," Gabe said from somewhere behind her.

She spun around. "Hi." She wanted to drop into his arms. Instead, she just shifted her weight from one foot to the other. "I had lunch with Tracy, my friend. We were talking about my mom's house."

"Did you get some news?"

"Not good news."

He backed away one step. "I'll call you in a minute."

What was he up to now? "Okay." She went back to her office and read over the work she'd finished that morning. It wasn't bad. But was it good enough to save her job?

About a half hour later, her phone rang. "Hi, sexy," Gabe drawled. "So, what has you looking so miserable?"

"My mom's house appraised twenty thousand dollars too low, and I don't have the cash to make up the difference."

"I can loan it to you."

"No way, but thank you."

"Why not?" He sounded hurt.

"That's really sweet. Thanks." She leaned back in her chair. "But what if something happens and I can't pay?"

"You'll pay it back."

"What if I'm fired? I won't be able to pay anything if I don't have a job."

"Would you quit with that? I told you, you're not going to get fired."

God, she wanted to believe him. "How can you be so sure? Duncan said they won't keep two marketing directors."

"He was just messing with you. He has a sick sense of humor."

No way. "Now, I know you're lying."

"I can't believe you just said that! Please, let me loan you the money."

"Why would you want to do that?"

"Because it would make me happy."

Oh Lord, he's going to make me cry. She closed her eyes and rubbed the tension from her neck. He was being so nice about this, still… No, she couldn't take his money.

"Fate, are you still there?"

"Yeah. Can you call me back in a few?"

"Sure. Bye."

She scribbled some figures. Mortgage, utilities, food, car payment, insurance… Her budget would be stretched to the upper limits, and she hadn't included a payment for his loan. Even if she took two years to repay it, she'd have to come up with a whopping eight hundred per month.

Impossible!

The phone rang, and she answered it. "Hello?"

"I've written the check."

"No!" She slumped forward, resting her chest on her desk. She had no energy.

"What's wrong?"

"I can't. I won't."

He sighed. "Okay, stubborn. Why not?"

"Even if I keep my job, I couldn't repay you."

"What if I helped you another way?"

"In what way?"

"A second job."

Now that suggestion had promise. "What kind of job?"

"Working for a friend of mine. It's a different kind of place. I'm not sure you'll like it, but he pays well."

"Just tell me I get to keep on my clothes."

He laughed. The sound was so soothing. "Hell, yes! I wouldn't send you to a place like that. Although, the way you stripped last night—"

Her face heated instantly. "Forget it! Now, tell me more about this other job."

"Well…what do you think about tattoos?"

"They're okay, I guess. But I'd never have one. Why? Do I have to get one?"

"No, but my friend owns a tattoo shop in downtown Royal Oak. He does tattoos and body piercing."

"Oh…" She knew it! Too good to be true. Conservative, squeamish, she'd never fit in at a place like that. "Maybe I'd better look for something else." *Like flipping burgers at a fast food restaurant.*

"Come on! Give it a try. You can handle one day, can't you? It's not like you'll be doing any tattooing or piercing. Just taking appointments over the phone, selling jewelry, that sort of thing. Like I said, the pay is great."

Why was it the man made the impossible sound logical? How did he do that?

She leaned back and tried to imagine the inside of a shop. Dark, smelly, smoky. Weird characters lying on tables. The buzz of tattoo guns—is that what they were called?—in the background. Selling kinky leather bodysuits and jewelry…

Actually, that part was kind of interesting.

"Okay. I'll give it a try. One day. If it doesn't work out, though, I won't go back. You'll warn him, right?"

"Already did. You start tomorrow morning. Ten sharp. You can thank me later." He chuckled.

She knew exactly what kind of thank-you he expected.

That sent another rush of heat to her face and between her legs. "Fair enough. And thanks. Seriously. I owe you."

"Not a problem. I told you, I care."

"I'm really starting to believe that."

"It's about time. Just remember, everything I do is for you. Now, where's my market analysis?"

"Right here on my desk."

"Excellent! I'll be there in one minute. That's the final section. I'll compile the whole thing this weekend and give Duncan a copy Monday morning. He likes to tweak things, change a word here and sentence there before it goes to the brass. Nothing major."

"Okay."

"You in the mood to celebrate tonight?"

She hadn't slept a wink last night, not after the way he'd rushed out. And her confusion had morphed into downright disappointment by morning, after hours and hours of stewing. "I'm kind of tired, to be honest."

"Okay," he huffed. "We can wait until tomorrow night. But I won't take no, so be prepared."

"That sounds great."

He hung up the phone, and as promised was at her door in two heartbeats. Her insides did a little dance when she opened the door and he flashed that million-dollar smile.

"Miss me?"

More than I'd ever admit. "Nope." She smiled and stepped aside to let him in. "But I think your tippy desk does."

"Yeah, old Bessy and me, we had a thing goin' there for a while." He stroked the desktop, and her insides melted as she watched the way his hands moved. They'd touched her the same way just last night...

She forced herself to walk around her desk, despite her legs being as soft as butter in the sun. "Here's the analysis."

"Great. Thanks, and good work. I couldn't have done better myself. We make a great team."

"I hope the suits see that."

He flopped into the chair on the other side of her desk. "They will. Now, quit worrying about it, would you?"

"Are you sure you don't need anything else from me? I don't think we've done the sales projections yet—"

"I took care of those. Go ahead, take it easy the rest of the afternoon."

"But I can't sit around here and do nothing. That'll only prove I'm not needed. You know, Duncan's right. After the company is launched, what would they need two marketing directors for?"

He leaned forward and reached for her cheek, palming it and thumbing her lips. She loved the way he touched her. "Has anyone told you that you worry too much?"

"Yes."

"Then, listen to them. I gotta go." Manila folder in hand, he stood and headed toward the door. "Oh," He stuffed his free hand in his pocket and handed her a card. Their fingertips brushed as the card was passed between them. "Here's the info on my buddy's place. Ten o'clock. Good luck tomorrow."

She watched him leave then glanced down. *Original Skin Tattoos.* "What is this? The "S" is a snake! She felt herself scowling as she stared at the card. "And look where the tongue is!"

"Yeah, Paul, the owner, has a great sense of humor, doesn't he?"

"Oh, just great." What in God's name was she thinking?

Chapter Ten
Sometimes guardian angels dress in camouflage.

The rest of the afternoon dragged by at a lame elephant's pace, thanks to the almost deafening silence in her office and the total lack of anything constructive to do. She tried to busy herself by reviewing old sales reports and scouring the phone book and newspaper for competitors' advertising. Michael didn't once stop in to see her.

He'd abandoned her.

She was a goner.

Maybe the tattoo place would be more of a savior than she'd originally planned. And so, after battling a mountain of reservation all afternoon, evening, night—yes, she couldn't sleep again!—and morning, she dressed in a pair of jeans and a t-shirt and drove to the heart of trendy Royal Oak. The shop was just south of the main drag, Main Street, where all the clothing, furniture shops, and restaurants were located. It sat inches from the road, no parking lot, so she parked around the corner on a side street. Once parked, she sucked in a few breaths and walked to the white house-turned-tattoo shop and headed inside.

Okay, the place didn't smell like she'd expected it to. And, for the most part it didn't look like she'd expected, either. It was clean, tidy, with two rows resembling dentist's chairs. What few patrons there were looked normal enough. The men's hair was a little longer than she was used to, and they wore a little more leather than she might see in a more conservative setting, but otherwise it seemed an okay place.

A young guy, built, with spikes sticking out of his lip, eyebrows and ears stepped up to the counter. "Hi, welcome to Original Skin. Can I help you?"

"I'm Fate. Gabe sent me."

"Fate!" He stuck out his hand, adorned on both inside and out with black ink. "Good to meet you. I'm Paul."

She took it and gave it a quick shake. "Good to meet you, Paul."

"Love the name, by the way. Did your parents give it to you, or did you choose it?" He gave her a friendly smile.

"No, I give my folks all the credit."

"Well, I'm sure you've guessed by now, this is my place. Most of the tattoos are done out here, and some piercing. The others, um...more personal ones are done in the private rooms in the back."

"Okay." She didn't want to imagine what that might entail.

"Do you have any tattoos?" He led her around the counter.

"No. I'm untouched...er, a tattoo virgin."

His gaze swept up and down her body. "Well, we just might have to change that."

She took a step backward. "What does that mean?"

He laughed. "I'm just kidding. I love to scare the shit out of the new help. Mark my words. After working here for a month, you'll have at least one."

"I doubt it."

He rattled his tongue ring in his mouth. "Either that, or you'll have one of these." He stuck out his tongue.

She cringed. "I definitely won't have one of those. To be honest, I don't see the big deal with them."

He laughed. "You will."

She didn't ask him what he meant by that.

"Okay. Well, you're in charge of taking phone calls, setting appointments. Here's the appointment book." He slid a large book in front of her. "It's pretty self-explanatory. Each of us has a column, and obviously you don't want to overlap appointments. Piercing takes fifteen minutes. Tattoos range depending on how intricate the design. People wanting a tattoo are first booked for a consultation and then they make an appointment for the artwork. Got it?"

Her head was swimming, but she was following so far. She nodded.

"Don't let the clients intimidate ya. Some of them are plain scary looking, but I guarantee they're a bunch of teddy bears."

"Okay."

"Any questions?"

"No... Oh, what time do I leave?"

"That anxious already?"

She glanced over and caught sight of a guy stabbing a needle through a young woman's belly. Her stomach turned. "No."

"You'll be fine. Just don't watch." He guided her back to the counter. "Stand here. Smile." He shoved a magazine at her. "Here, you can even read this to pass the time. We won't get busy 'til later. And you're done at seven. You can take lunch whenever you like. Just let me know before you leave."

"Okay." Lunch? If she watched another mini-sword slice through skin, she doubted she'd be able to hold down a bite.

The young woman zipped up her pants, cringing, and headed for the door.

Why the hell would anyone do that to themselves?

She opened the magazine. The first picture was of a singing star wearing a crop top and hip hugger jeans. A red jewel glittered in her belly button. Okay, maybe that was a little sexy...

Another young woman walked in, sending the little bell tied to the door into a fit of tinkles. The woman approached the counter.

"Hi, may I help you?" Fate asked.

"I'd like to get a body piercing."

"Okay. Let me just check our book, see when we'll have someone available. What sort of piercing would you like?"

"My nipples."

"Oh." She fought the urge to cringe. *Yikes!* "Looks like someone is available now. Let me just verify. If you'd like, you can take a look at the jewelry while you wait."

"Okay. Thanks."

Fate stepped from the counter and made a beeline for Paul's last known location, through the back door. But as she opened it, she realized it led to a narrow corridor lined on either side by doors. Which one?

She knocked on the first door.

A man completely full of tattoos, bushy beard and piercings, popped his head out. "What do you want?"

"Sorry. Wrong room. Do you happen to know where Paul might be?"

"Last door on the left."

"Thanks."

He closed the door and she headed down the corridor and knocked.

"Come in."

She hesitated for a split second while a rush of images flashed through her brain. Women lying prostrate with rings and studs everywhere...

"Come in," he repeated.

The door opened, revealing Paul...and a desk.

Big relief!

"There's a woman wanting a body piercing, and your schedule is free. Do you want to take her?"

"Sure. I'll be there in a minute. Help her select the jewelry. She'll need at least fourteen gauge."

She had no clue what he meant, but she'd figure it out. "All right." She returned to find the woman holding a pair of gold hoops. Just out of curiosity, she took the jewelry from the woman and read the cards in the tiny plastic envelopes. It said fourteen G. Guess that was what he'd meant.

She smiled. "Paul will be with you in just a moment."

The woman nodded. She looked a little pale.

Fate stepped behind the counter and watched the woman as she wandered the small lobby area. "Are you okay?"

"Yeah, I'm fine. A little nervous."

A little? She looked like she might pass out. And he hadn't done a thing to her yet. "I would be too."

"Do you have any piercings?"

"Nope. I'm scared of needles."

Paul approached, introduced himself and, chattering in a friendly voice, led the ghost-white young woman away. About fifteen minutes later, he rushed up to Fate's desk. "I need some sugar. Can you hand me a sucker from the bottom drawer?"

"Are you having a sugar fix?"

"No, Tina, the little lady with the nipple piercing, is about to pass out. A boost of sugar'll bring her 'round."

Why would anyone do this to herself? She rummaged through the drawer, finally finding a root beer Dum-Dum sucker. "There you go."

Moments later the pale girl sat on a chair in the lobby, slurping on that sucker. Her face slowly morphed from grayish to pink. And she left.

Never! Never in a million years would Fate do such a thing. She shook her head.

For the next several hours, she greeted patients—if that was what they were called—of all kinds. Some young kids with altered drivers licenses—she learned real quick how to pick up those. Most of the people seemed to handle whatever procedure they had done well. Fate refused to watch the actual event, knowing she'd never come back if she did.

She wasn't sure she would anyway. This place just wasn't her thing.

The final hours passed quicker than the earlier ones, thanks to a rush of people. Before she knew it, it was time to close.

"See you tomorrow?" Paul asked as she removed the cash from the register and put it in a bank bag.

"I don't—"

The doorbell tinkled, and she automatically blurted, "Sorry, we're closed." She looked up.

Gabe! Thank God! A familiar face. A bit of sanity in an insane place.

"How'd she do?" he asked Paul.

"Great. Hope she'll come back."

"She will." Gabe tossed an arm over her shoulders and gave them a squeeze. "She's a trooper."

A trooper? Well, she might be that. But she wasn't sure she was the body piercing-slash-tattoo-parlor receptionist they needed. "Actually—"

"She'll see you tomorrow at ten," Gabe interrupted.

"Would you let me finish?" she whispered.

"No, because I know what you're going to say. Let's go get something to eat, and we'll talk about it."

More than a little annoyed, she followed him outside. "Look, I appreciate everything you've done, but you're being too pushy. I like to make my own decisions, thank you."

"You need the job, right? Where else are you going to make two hundred dollars a week, cash, in two days?"

"Two hundred?"

"Yeah. Didn't he tell you?"

"No. I figured I'd get maybe seven an hour."

He kissed her nose, and her insides turned to warm mush. "You're a cutie."

She gave him a shove. "No, I'm not. I'm an intelligent, independent woman, and don't you forget that. But yes, thank you very much, I'm cute."

They walked to a nearby restaurant so loaded with people it felt like they were standing front row at a crowded rock concert. Music blaring from hidden speakers and the loud chattering of boisterous diners melded into a deafening chaos. "Can we go somewhere quieter?" she shouted.

"Sure." He took her hand and led her outside.

Much better!

They grabbed an outside table at the next restaurant, a cozy Italian place, and after ordering their drinks, settled into a comfortable conversation. She shared her experiences from her first day on the job, and he encouraged her to continue, reminding her that the first day of any job was always the worst and the pay was great.

"I still don't get the body piercing thing." She sipped her diet cola. "It looks so...painful."

"It doesn't really hurt as bad as you think. Not if it's done right."

She shook her head. There was no way he'd convince her.

He smiled. "Maybe someday you'll get your bellybutton pierced. I think that's incredibly sexy." He licked his lips.

Now, that was a sight. His tongue working on anything sent heat straight to her groin. "I saw a picture. It is cute—if you have a nice stomach." No way in hell she'd let Paul or anyone else shove a needle through her tummy!

His eyebrows lifted, and an eager smile spread over his face. "Then you'll do it?"

"Not a chance." She hated disappointing him. That expression was almost enough to get her to reconsider.

"Damn!" He pouted for a fraction of a second. "Well, at least you're going to go back tomorrow, right?"

"I don't know…"

He tipped his head like a puppy. "I'll write the check for the house…all you have to do is pay me back…one hundred a week is good—"

"Okay! I surrender!" She waved her hands before her. "I'll go back. But if I hate it, I'm quitting."

"Fair enough. Now that we have that covered, let's go to the next subject." He gave her a crooked grin.

She had an inkling what that meant. "And what subject might that be?"

The waitress delivered their food, and they waited for her to finish doling out the plates before continuing their conversation.

"You were saying?" she prodded.

"Sleeping arrangements?"

Her whole body flamed. "Oh?"

"Your place or mine? In fact, I'm not all that hungry. Do you want to take this home by any chance?"

"Sure, we can do that." Shit! She was soooo starving, saliva was pooling under her tongue.

He flagged down the waitress and asked for boxes and the check.

She watched him, suspicious. "What are you up to?"

"Nothing. Just want some privacy, that's all."

She didn't believe that for a minute. But she was mildly curious—no, she was very curious—so she played along. She packed her delicate, lonely, scrumptious chicken and pasta into the Styrofoam box and followed him from the restaurant. They held hands as they walked to her car, and he gave her a long, enthusiastic kiss at the curb.

After she got into her car and started it, he ducked down and stuck his head in her open window. "I'll follow you back to your place, okay?"

"Okay. See you there."

She drove the short distance home, losing him at a traffic light. But she knew he could find his way. She was in a hurry. The food sitting in her passenger seat was sending tidal waves of saliva into her mouth. She swallowed for the umpteenth time. If he kissed her again, it would be one wet and sloppy kiss.

When she parked, she went into the house, dumped her food onto a plate and nuked it. When the timer chimed, Gabe knocked on the front door.

She shoved a forkful into her mouth and headed to the door.

Good God! He was such a handsome man. And somehow, during that short drive over, he'd gotten almost completely undressed.

Oh yeah, what a sight…! Eek, someone will see him.

She chewed, swallowed, and gripped him by the wrist and yanked him inside. "What are you doing? You'll get a ticket being in public like that!"

"I'm wearing shorts—"

"Boxers, you moron! Underwear." *Nice ones too.* She touched them. "Silk?"

"Only the best for you."

She rolled her eyes. "Please. Save the clichés. Where's your dinner? Did you leave it in the car?"

"Oh! Yeah. I'll go out—" He spun around and pulled open the door.

"Like hell you will." She pushed past him. "I'll get it. You stay put. I don't want the neighbors getting an eyeful. They're nosy enough." She went to his car and opened the passenger side door.

And stopped cold. A huge box sat in the seat. White, tied with a big red ribbon. Flowers. She grabbed it, and the dinner sitting on the floor, and headed inside.

"Damn! I knew I should have left those at home." Gabe smacked his forehead. "They're for my next-door neighbor. Her mother died."

He didn't actually expect her to believe that, did he? His silly grin was a giveaway. Nope. "You're…sweet." She carried the box to the kitchen and rummaged in the back of her cupboard for a vase. Then she opened the box. The fragrance alone was something to behold! And the flowers…so many! Beautiful red roses trimmed with green stuff and baby's breath. "Thanks! They're gorgeous. What did I do to deserve these?"

"Read the card."

She picked up the business card-sized envelope and opened it. "Thanks for giving me a second chance. Love, Gabe," she read aloud. "Wow. I don't know what to say."

"Are you happy?" He stepped closer, and her body reacted instantly. Her heart skittered in her chest. Her face heated. Her mouth went dry.

She thought about his question for a moment.

Despite all the turmoil, she had to admit it, she was happy. Very happy. "Yes."

He gathered her into his arms and kissed her, soft and seductive at first, and then intense and demanding the next. And she met each thrust of his tongue with one of her own. Her body melded to his form, her legs straddling his, her breasts flattened against his ribcage, her hands exploring his shoulders, chest and stomach.

He broke the kiss. "Now, let's eat! I'm starving."

In the next breath, she was left standing in the middle of the kitchen, her head swimming.

He picked up his carton and walked to the living room, forking beef-something into his mouth. She watched him for a moment, mesmerized by the way his muscles moved under his skin. He had one hell of a body.

Fork in mouth, he plopped onto the couch. "Do you have a remote?" His feet rested on the coffee table.

"Yep. On the side table." She pointed then took up her plate and sat beside him. Together they watched an old black and white flick with Fred and Ginger.

This was it! What life should be like. Never before had the simple things been so much fun. Just sitting there, eating cold food, Gabe next to her, poking fun at the old movie. She could live like this forever.

When she'd crammed as much food as she dared into her stomach, she put the rest away for tomorrow and headed to the bathroom to freshen up. If he was going to spend the night, certain preparations were in order. First, she ran bath water. Hot. Lots of fragrant bath oil. She stripped and eased herself in.

Ahhh...

A knock sounded at the bathroom door. "Mind if I join you?"

"Not at all."

He opened the door. "You looked lonely. I might be persuaded into taking a bubble bath. Is there room for two?"

"Sure." She sat forward, and he removed the only remaining garment he was wearing and sat behind her. Then she leaned back and rested against him.

He reached around, took the pink scrubby from her and filled it full of fragrant bath gel then gave her back a friendly shove. "Lean forward. I'll wash you."

"Do I stink?" she teased, relishing the way his hands freely explored her body.

"Not at all. But I want to give you the full treatment."

Those words held *such* promise. "What would that entail?"

"You'll just have to wait to find out." He pressed her again, and she leaned forward.

The slight abrasion of the pink netting felt so good, and the tiny kisses that followed in its wake felt even better. She was getting hot. In a lukewarm tub! She raised her hands to her face.

"Are you all right?"

"Sure. The water's just a little hot, I think."

"Are you positive that's all it is?" He pulled her shoulders back until she was resting against his chest and stomach again. His arms wrapped around her and he paid special attention to her breasts. Fingertips teased each nipple to aching erection. Her knees fell open, when he breathed deeply.

Damn, she wanted him! She wanted to remain in some control, but that familiar throbbing ache settled between her legs.

And then he pushed her forward, stood, stepped out of the tub and swooped her up in his arms. *My hero!* He was so strong. She loved the feeling of utter vulnerability. It was incredibly sexy. He carried her into the bedroom and dropped her onto the bed. "I don't want to wait another minute. And I have a surprise for you."

Lava-hot blood shot through her whole body. "What kind of surprise?"

He pulled her legs until her ass was at the edge of the bed. Then he smiled, parted her knees and...and...*Holy shit!* She never cursed.

What was that?

Her clit was throbbing. Something was rubbing it in flickering motions. Something hard. Something incredible. What the hell? Her mind went blank. Every muscle in her body tensed as she was swept into a wild orgasm that shook her whole body. It was the most intense explosion. Her inner muscles pulsed as he slid a finger inside. "Oh, yeah."

And then he thrust his hard cock inside, filling her so completely she could cry. He moved slowly at first, as the last few seconds of her orgasm passed. And then he hammered her. Deep and hard. She felt a second orgasm coming, felt the heat shoot out from her center to every part of her. Felt the overpowering wave.

He groaned low as he came. That extra fullness sent her over the edge again, and she rode him, reached up and clung to his arms as her body convulsed and twitched and eventually relaxed.

He pulled out and climbed into bed with her.

"What was that?" she asked, still trying to catch her breath.

He smiled. "What?"

"What you did to me? It was incredible."

He stuck his tongue out. A silver ball sat in the middle.

"You?"

He waggled his eyebrows. "Fun, isn't it?"

"I had no idea."

"Why do you think they're so popular?"

"To look cool?" She knew she sounded stupid, but she'd never thought much about it.

He laughed and gave her a squeeze. "There are so many things—wonderful, sexy, wild things—I can't wait to show you."

She sighed. "Mmmm. Sounds good. Lead the way. When do we begin?"

"Right now, if you want."

She sighed. "I want."

He grinned like a kid with a new toy. "Be right back." He jumped up, grabbed her robe off the hook on the closet door, and wrapped it around himself.

He looked pretty damn cute in the short, pink terrycloth number. Another man might have looked ridiculous, but Gabe, even in pink terrycloth looked like such *a man*, so virile.

Moments later, her front door thumped closed, and she heard the deadbolt hit home.

And within another couple of heartbeats he was standing at the foot of her bed with a giant duffle bag.

"What's that? Your clothes?" She leaned up on her elbows.

"Nope." His grin was as wicked as a grin could get. "My toys."

That expression was almost a little scary. "What kind of toys?"

"You'll see—um, kinda—in a minute. You trust me, don't you?"

"Well..." Her still thrumming pussy clenched in response yet a part of her hesitated. She did trust him, didn't she? He hadn't done anything to her that she hadn't wanted. Quite the opposite, actually. So why the twinge of apprehension? Because this was Gabe.

"This'll really test your trust." He dropped the bag on the floor and unzipped it.

She crawled to the foot of the bed to see what he was doing.

He pushed her back. "Uh uh. No peeking. Now. Sit on the edge of the bed."

The authority in his voice sent another shockwave through her body. She felt herself heating up from the inside out as she scooted to the edge. A game! She'd never played a sex game before.

"Close your eyes."

She closed her eyes, and was surprised when his first touch was on her face.

He tied a blindfold over her eyes. "How's that?" He tugged at the corners and around her nose.

Oh... This was going to be one of *those* games.

She'd never played submissive before. "I can't see a thing." Her pussy slicked in anticipation as images of him teasing and spanking her shot through her mind.

"Excellent. Now," he said in her ear. "The good stuff begins." Those words pummeled her body, sending more juices to her pussy.

He forced her shoulders down on the bed and opened her legs. And with no warning, he parted her labia and lapped at her clit, slow, torturous circles that sent wave after wave of need through her body. All her muscles tensed as blood pumped through her at lightening speed. He nipped her clit, and a sharp blade of pleasure-pain shot up her spine. A finger delved into her sodden pussy, pumping in and out, in and out, and she opened her legs wider for him, wishing his cock would fill her completely.

Her breathing came in short bursts as she felt herself hurtling toward climax.

And then he stopped.

Her muscles instantly relaxed.

She heard the sound of metal, clicking, sliding. *What the...?*

He gripped her thigh and lifted it high, pressing her leg back toward her chest. He strapped something around it then did the same with the other leg. Next, he lifted her arms overhead and tied them wide apart.

Oh God! She was as exposed as she'd be on a gyno table, her legs spread, knees high, her pussy cooled by the air drifting down from the ceiling fan.

And she was as hot as she could be. Totally, completely turned on.

Then, her ass was lifted up and a pillow of some sort was slid under her. Now, her head was lower than her ass, her back resting on some sort of angled cushion.

She waited, listening, awash in anticipation and a tiny sliver of apprehension as he rummaged around in his bag of tricks. Her heart thumped in her chest, her senses alert to every sound and smell.

"Have you ever been fucked with a dildo?" he whispered.

His question sent an appealing image through her mind. Once, she'd had a friend who worked at one of those stores—the kind that sold sex toys and movies. She couldn't begin to compute the times she'd almost gone in there to buy one but turned around at the last minute. She was such a coward. "Um. No."

He chuckled.

Suddenly, those bindings felt just a little too tight, and her pussy felt just a little too open.

She felt something touching her stomach. Her muscles twitched under the soft touch, and goose bumps erupted over her skin. Her knees lowered.

"Don't move or you'll be sorry."

She stopped. The way her pussy was throbbing, she knew he was right.

He pushed her knees back. "Leave them like this."

Something touched her mouth. Soft. She licked, tasting him and a hint of herself. "Take me in your mouth."

She opened wide and swallowed, suckling, her tongue pressed down against the bottom of her mouth by his width. He pulled out and she teased the head with her tongue, scraping her teeth over the velvety flesh until he groaned.

And then he was gone again. "For that, you get a reward."

Her pussy juices streamed at the promise in those words.

The first touch was to her inner thigh. Something hard.

Snap.

It buzzed, sending deep vibrations into her thigh muscles. As he moved it up, her stomach muscles clenched. The vibrator slowly, torturously slid between her legs, skirted around her pussy, up over her pubic bone and then down the other leg.

That was a reward? Not in her book! That was more like a punishment. "Hey, about twelve inches higher, please!"

"You're not complaining?" The vibrator disappeared. "Are you?"

Man, he was tough. "No."

"I'm still not convinced."

She forced herself to sound genuine. "No, I'm not complaining."

She heard the hum again, and she felt herself smiling.

This time, it found its start at her stomach and traveled up, first to buzz over one nipple, bringing it to a quick erection, and then the other.

"Your body is so eager to please. I like that." His voice was low, the sound of it humming through her like the vibrations of the sex toy.

He parted her ass cheeks and set the buzzing vibrator there, teasing her anus and pressing softly. She forced herself to relax, welcoming the vibrations inside as the vibrator delved deep.

Slam. Her body pulsed with an instant climax. Her ass throbbed, the muscles clenching and unclenching around the vibrator. Her arms and legs spasmed. Her lungs froze, and then she gasped for air. Her head swam.

"Mmmm." He pulled the vibrator away. "What a good girl you are. I can't wait to see what you do next."

Next? He was going to do more? She was sure she'd die. Was sure every bit of energy she possessed had been spent. She was weak to the core, her pussy so inflamed she feared even the slightest touch would send bolts of white heat up her spine. "Please, no more."

"What did you say?" His voice had lost all the rich, velvety smoothness it had possessed just a heartbeat ago.

"I can't."

"I'll tell you what you can or cannot do." He kissed her neck. "I've been easy on you. I didn't even make you call me master, yet."

"Yet?"

He chuckled, nibbling on her ear. "I know how much you love domination games."

"You do? I do?" Okay, so what if he was teasing. She'd come—what? Two, three times? She'd never done that before. How could she possibly come again so soon? Her pussy was tired. Her ass was sore. Her arms and legs were trembling. Her mind was lost forever in a bog. "I think it's been incredible. I mean, I've never... But now, I've had enough. Let's cuddle. Multiple orgasms can be exhausting."

"Exhausting? You mean this was grueling for you? I've taken my time pleasuring you, and you haven't appreciated it?" he asked in a teasing voice.

"I have. It was great—better than great—but I'm tired."

"Okay." He let out an exaggerated sigh. "But I withhold the right to change your mind."

She almost wondered what that meant. She couldn't come up with a response.

Another touch, soft and tickly started at the insides of her knees, and unbelievably, her pussy came alive again. It tightened and slicked.

"How's that?" He was close, his breath in her ear. He kissed her, his mouth tasting of her essence. It was sweet, mellow. His tongue slid into her mouth as his lips moved slowly over hers. It was a wonderfully erotic kiss, lazy, yet promising.

She moaned into his mouth, the sound echoing in her head. She felt another wave of heat settling between her legs.

And then she felt the lightest touch there, parting her lips and sliding up to her clit. When it hit its mark, her stomach muscles contracted, tilting her pelvis up toward the source of the touch. Slow, smooth circles traveled down around her vagina and up over her clit. Around and around, teasing her until she thought she'd have to beg for him to touch her inside.

But he had mercy, and slipped a finger inside, hooking it to touch the sensitive spot on the top inner wall.

"Oh…" She didn't know she could react yet again, but there she was, knees up around her chin, her thigh muscles tight, her pussy wet and ready, all in response to what that man did with his mouth and hand. She was there again, soaring toward another climax. A wash of heat shot out from her center, reaching every minute part of her.

He stopped.

Oh no! That wasn't fair. He'd gotten her all riled up again. Surely he wasn't that cruel.

"Okay. Well, I guess I'm through now. Are you ready to be untied?"

No! "But. But I liked what you were doing. I was close." It wasn't easy talking in this position. In fact, she felt downright sluttish. Who ever heard of a woman spread open like this having to beg for it?

"I thought you were too tired."

"No, I just thought I was." He was going to make her beg! If she wasn't so damn horny at the moment, she just might…do something, like hit him over the head. "Please?"

"Please what?" His voice was teasing. He was having fun with this? Jerk!

"Please fuck me," she growled, adding a little intentional desperation for his pleasure. Anything to get that huge cock inside her to finish the job. Her body hummed from head to toe. She had a feeling this climax would be the best ever.

Without warning, he plunged inside, filling her. She yelped in both surprise and pleasure and gripped the coverlet in her hands as she braced herself for some real, down-and-dirty fucking. That was the only word for it.

He didn't fool with the slow stuff, went right for a fast, hard hammering. And her body—every inch of it—appreciated the movement. She rocked her hips in time with him, taking him in as deep as she could. Every muscle in her body strained as more heat flashed over her. She felt the tingly sensation of an approaching orgasm.

And then, for a split second, she felt the added girth of his impending orgasm. It, and his finger rotating over her clit, pushed her over the edge and sent her soaring through a curtain of red and yellow light. Every part of her shuddered, her pussy milking every last drop of come from him.

He growled low like a bear. "Damn, woman!"

It didn't stop, that incredible, unbelievable pulsing as she continued soaring. He slowed his movement, his cock twitching inside. And as he did, her orgasm eased, leaving her completely drunk, in a natural high.

He pulled out, and she cried out in protest. "Shhh." He untied the blindfold, and she blinked at the dim light of her bedside lamp.

Fighting an urge to sleep like she'd never known, hardly able to keep her eyelids up, she smiled at him then glanced down at herself, bound, a metal bar between her thighs, held by black straps. It was a wild sight, and one that made her horny all over again.

Who would've thought she'd get into stuff like that?

He freed her from the bar, and the other one holding her wrists, and they snuggled in bed. She closed her eyes, relishing the smell of him, the sound of his slow breathing. The feel of his arm wrapped protectively around her shoulders, and the lingering twitches of her last orgasm.

"So, what did you think of that?" he asked, a tiny sparkle of laughter in his voice.

She forced herself to sound nonchalant. "I guess I could keep you around for a while."

He jacked himself up on an elbow and looked her in the eye, one finger under her chin. "You'd better. I know you're too smart to throw away a man who would do anything in the world for you."

"Would you?"

"Haven't I proven that already?"

"Well, I have to admit, you've been really sweet. The job. Offering to loan me that money. I've never had a boyfriend be so generous before."

"Boyfriend? Did you just call me your boyfriend?" He beamed.

She kissed the tip of his nose. "I suppose I can't call you my enemy anymore. And friend just doesn't fit."

"I'll take boyfriend, though I'd prefer fiancé."

"You haven't asked me to marry you yet." She motioned toward her ring finger, surprised the conversation had taken such a serious turn so quickly. Did he really mean what he said? Could he really want to marry her? After such a short time?

He smacked his forehead. "Yeah. Guess I'm jumping the gun just a bit there."

"I mean. We haven't known each other...well, we have, but we haven't. Oh, darn. What do I mean to say?"

"I think you're scared shitless. But, sweetheart. That's all right. I can take my time. Prove myself. In the end, you'll be mine. That's all I care about."

"I hope you mean that. I really do. It just takes me a while. I've had such rotten luck with men."

"That's because you and I were destined to be together. No other man was good enough."

She chuckled. The man was confident if nothing else. "Oh, so now you're a prophet?"

"Prophet. Guardian angel. And marketing guru. Yep. That's me." He thumped his chest. "And all yours, baby. I'll never do anything to hurt you. I mean it, Fate. I love you."

Love.

She fell asleep with that word echoing through her head, his arms around her shoulders, his cock resting against her ass, and a smile on her face.

Chapter Eleven
Hell is just around the corner from paradise.

They must have made love at least a dozen times. By the end of the weekend, Fate was worn out, but completely, absolutely, utterly fulfilled. That man was a sex machine, and she loved every minute of it.

In fact, his enthusiasm left her feeling sexy, daring and downright naughty—in a good way. Who would believe that she, Fate the conservative, could be Fate the sexy vixen? She couldn't wait until next weekend, since they'd promised to take it easy Monday through Friday, for work's sake.

Monday morning, she cast aside Sunday's impulsive decision to call in sick and dressed, leaving her hair down, since Gabe said it was sexy, and went to work. Her spirits were somewhere up in the clouds, despite having spent a second day at the tattoo parlor and witnessing more body piercing than she'd ever wished to see in a lifetime.

Yes, life was good. Her mother's house was nearly hers. All she had to do was make the phone call to the bank to authorize the loan processing. Gabe was hers. He'd said he loved her. He'd proven he loved her, over and over and over again.

Nothing—short of being fired—would rain on her parade today.

She went to her office and sat at her desk.

Where was her mail?

Where was Michael? He always had it there for her, first thing. Sheesh! The man had forsaken her completely. What was that all about?

The phone rang, and she answered it, expecting Gabe's friendly voice.

"Fate?"

"Michael? Where are you? Didn't you come to work today?"

"We need to talk."

Those words always filled her with dread. "What's wrong?"

"Meet me for lunch at the cafeteria next door, okay?"

An ugly feeling crawled up her spine. "What's going on? Can't you tell me over the phone?"

"No. I want to tell you in person. I'll let you get back to work. See you soon."

Click. Buzz.

What the hell?

She went out to the main bank of cubicles. Maybe Gabe knew something. She couldn't concentrate until she knew exactly what was going on.

Gabe's cubicle was empty. Damn! Where was he? Michael was gone. Gabe, too. Were they planning something? A joke maybe? Gabe was a schemer. He just might be...

Her mind shooting off into a million different directions, she wandered back to her office and shut the door. But instead of ruminating, she forced herself to get busy. Her first task, call the bank and get the loan underway. That finished, she reached for her active files, what little she had.

Gone. Her files were gone? Her whole file cabinet was empty.

Oh, God! Had they called her and left a message on her answering machine? Had they fired her? She could understand a few files being missing. Gabe could have needed those for the report. But all of them?

She felt sick. Dizzy.

Arms out, hands on the desktop, she steadied herself and stood. And then she stormed from her office, making a beeline for the one place she knew she could get answers. Duncan's office.

She knocked.

No answer.

She tried the door. Locked.

Where to now? She rushed downstairs to the conference room and hearing voices, she opened the door.

Like one of those computer-aided missiles, her gaze went straight to Gabe, standing at the front before a screen, their report, larger than life, lit up from an overhead projector.

"What the hell?" she said.

Gabe set down his pointer and rushed toward her. But suddenly aware of all the people sitting at the long conference table with eyes on her, she turned and left the room. She was lost. Didn't know where to go.

"I know it looks bad—" Gabe said behind her.

She spun around. "It sure does. Can you explain why I shouldn't be panicking right now? What is this? What are you doing in there? I thought we were supposed to make the presentation together. You and me. A team, remember? What the hell is going on?" Her nose burned. No way! She wouldn't cry. She sniffed.

"Duncan dropped it on me this morning, and I didn't tell you because you said you weren't coming in today."

"You suggested I take the day..." Oh, no! This situation had the distinct stench of deceit. "What else don't I know?"

He visibly swallowed. "A lot."

The conference room door opened, and Duncan joined them in the hall, his gaze hopping back and forth between them. "Is there a problem out here?"

"Nope." Gabe shook his head.

"Yes, there is." Why was he acting this way? "Gabe, why didn't you want me here today? At least you can let me come in and finish the presentation."

"Please, Fate, let's talk about this later." He turned to Duncan. "I'll be right there."

Duncan glanced at his wristwatch. "You better. You know Bradford has a plane to catch."

"Yep. One minute."

Duncan nodded and returned to the conference room, closing the door behind him.

Gabe caught Fate's upper arms. "Listen. I promise we'll talk. Just let me finish the presentation. I'll come find you as soon as I'm done."

She ripped herself free from his grasp. This wasn't happening! He wasn't giving her the brush off. He hadn't taken her job from her, had he? Oh hell! "Good luck finding me. You lying, scheming..." Shit there wasn't an ugly enough word for him. "I can't believe I was so stupid! Shit! You give me a little cock, and I'm ready to roll over and let you shove it up my ass. So, I suppose I don't have a job anymore—except for the pathetic job at the tattoo parlor...oh, my God! You've known about this for a lot longer than you said, didn't you?"

"I'll tell you later. Please!"

She turned from him, couldn't stand looking at that lying face for another second. What an idiot she'd been. So swept up in dreams of love—love! What a joke!—she'd missed what he was doing right under her nose.

Never again!

She went back to her office—correction, his office—and packed up her few personal belongings, and she was out the door within minutes.

She had no idea where to go. It was much too early to meet Michael for lunch. Michael! She scrolled down to his name on her cell phone and hit the call button.

He picked up on the second ring.

"Michael, it's Fate. Are you busy right now?" She felt a sob sitting in her gut. She forced it to stay down there.

"No. Do you want to meet earlier?"

"Yes." Her eyes watered, and she couldn't see. Still, she kept walking to her car. She ran the back of her hand across her eyes and blinked to clear them. "Somewhere close by..."

"Where are you?"

"Parking lot."

"Okay. I'll meet you at the Star Restaurant, down the street. You know where it is?"

"Yes." Her hip struck a truck bumper, and she swallowed a yelp. She blinked a few more times.

"Hang in there, Fate. I'll see you in a few."

"Thanks." Finding her car, she hit the end button and ran to it, sat, and cried until there weren't any more tears left. How had things gone so wrong in such a short time? How had she been so blind?

Almost composed enough to function, she started her car and drove the short distance to the restaurant. Her legs felt funny, squishy, rubbery, as she walked. Yet, they propelled her forward. She had to know the truth, had to confirm her suspicions, even though it would…it would just about kill her.

Another sob shot up her throat.

She yanked open the door, caught Michael's gaze, so full of guilt and regret it could have been written in red ink across his face, and turned tail. She couldn't hear this in a public place.

"Fate!" Michael called after her. "I'm so sorry."

"Why are you apologizing?" She didn't turn around to face him but kept walking to her car. She pulled open the door. "What part did you play in all this?"

"They used me too. Just like you."

She sat, feet on the concrete, knees sticking out the car, and looked up.

Michael looked like he might cry. "They are a bunch of bastards. Every one of them."

"Tell me."

He hunkered down and took his hands in hers. "I had no idea what they were up to. Gabe told me to stick with him, and I'd be okay—more than okay. He said I'd get a promotion." He sighed. "I was such an idiot, Fate. I swallowed his lies, hook, line and sinker. Then this morning, Kathy from Human Resources called me at home and told me I was fired. Just like that! I still can't believe it."

"They fired you?"

He nodded. "Told me I'd get an official notice in a couple of days. Kathy apologized. She sounded mad, like she didn't appreciate the way they were handling me."

"Well, that is pretty low. No company I've ever worked for fired people over the phone."

"Tell me about it! I'm still trying to figure out what happened." He fell back on his rump, and she realized the expression she'd seen earlier wasn't what she thought. He was dazed, overwhelmed, not guilty. "I know they are firing you, too. Gabe more or less told me that by insisting I stay in his camp. It killed me watching him sweet-talk you the way he did. He told me if I said a word to you, both of us would be fired on the spot. And since I knew about your house problem, I didn't want to take the chance..." His gaze dropped to the ground. "Damn it, I should have told you so you'd be prepared."

"You did what you thought was best, for my sake." Her head was still reeling, unable to fully comprehend what she was hearing. "So, Gabe was behind all of this? He was scheming behind my back? Planning to take over my job?" God, it hurt like hell to say those things! "I can't believe I was so blind."

And how would she break the news to her mother? She couldn't get the mortgage without a job. The house would be auctioned in days.

Damn!

Her cell phone rang and she swept it up and glanced at the display. "Speak of the devil!" Her heart jumped, and hot blood pounded in her temples. She punched the call button. "Gabe, what do you want?"

"A chance to explain."

"Go to hell."

"You don't know the whole story."

"I don't want to. Go to hell, you lying piece of garbage. And don't ever call me again." She hesitated for a moment, wondering if there might, somehow, despite the way things looked, be another side to this whole thing.

Stupid, blind hope! She punched the button, cutting him off.

After tossing her phone on the dashboard, she turned her attention back to Michael, a man who looked as defeated as she felt. "You're a fantastic assistant. I'm sure you can find another job."

"I've called every placement agency in the tri-county area. They're all giving me the same story, the economy's slow right now but they'll keep my resume on file."

"Crap!" She slammed her hands on the steering wheel. "If I were a vengeful person, I'd do something to get back at that bastard. Something really nasty."

"But you're not. And I'm not. And we'll both carry on." He rubbed her arm. "It was great working with you, Fate Doherty. You're one in a million." He stood, turned and walked away.

"Yeah, one of the stupidest people out of a million." She started her car and drove down the street. Best to get it over with and go tell her mother.

And, just for the hell of it, she called John and made a lunch date for tomorrow. If nothing else, a friendly face might keep her from falling apart...completely.

* * * * *

Gabe tried her cell phone again. Busy. Damn! "I told you she'd come in today," he said to Duncan, who stood in his doorway, leaning against the frame. Stupid ass! He never should have agreed to this! He'd been so close to gaining her complete trust. "I'll never get a chance to explain, now."

"Forget her. We don't need her anyway. I only agreed with your crazy suggestion because I wanted to keep you."

"Well, maybe I should quit too." His heart pounded so hard in his chest, he was sure his ribcage would explode. "She needs this job!"

"Well, I couldn't help it. Bradford's leaving today. We couldn't wait any longer. It's purely business—"

"To hell with business! And to hell with Bradford. This is his fifth marriage. It'll end before he returns home from his honeymoon. To hell with this whole frickin' place. Bunch of pompous assholes." He hurled the Single Temptation binder across the room. It hit the wall with a loud thump, leaving a nice triangular dent in the drywall before landing on Gabe's old metal desk.

"Hey, I can understand why you're upset, but that's no way to talk about—"

"You have no idea why I'm upset, and you couldn't give a shit."

"That's not true." Duncan bent down and wagged a forefinger in front of Gabe's nose. "I put up with your bullshit for a long time, even put my own ass on the line so you could get a little pussy. Now, be a man, take the disappointment and go on with your life. And for God's sake, have a little pride. Don't do anything stupid. And don't go crawling back to her, begging for forgiveness. You'll never get it."

"She thinks I lied to her. Used her. Manipulated her. And if she talks to Michael, she could think even worse. I have to find her somehow, make her listen—"

Duncan straightened to his full height and shook his head. "She'll never believe you."

"She has to. I'll make her, somehow."

"She's not the kind to be made to do anything."

"Yeah. I know. That's why I love her."

Duncan shook his head and walked back to the door. "You're lost, pussy-whipped. I never thought I'd see the day."

"I'm not lost. I've learned what's important in life. Maybe someday you will too." He stood, charged past the clueless man and headed out the door.

"You'd better be back here by—"

"I'll come back if and when I feel like it." He dashed down the stairs, across the lobby, and outside. "Now, if I were a pissed off Fate Doherty, where would I be?" He started his car and headed south toward her place, doubtful he'd find her there, but hoping he might.

And of course, she wasn't home.

Parked in her driveway, he dialed her cell phone again. This time, he got her voice mail. "Hi, Fate. I can imagine what you're thinking, but please listen. I did this all for you. Please. Believe me. Let me explain. I did it all for you. I love you. I want to marry you." He punched the end button and drove home.

He'd lost her. The only person in the world that mattered. "Shit!"

Chapter Twelve
*Sometimes it's easier to believe the worst
about someone than the best.*

Fate checked the recent calls on her cell. Gabe, again? Would he never give up? That was the last human being she wanted to talk to at the moment.

She punched the power button, got out of the car, and escorted her mother to the front door. "We shouldn't be doing this. What if someone calls the police?"

"No one will, honey. I just have to get one last look. You understand, don't you?" Standing on the front porch, her mother swept her arms in a wide arc. "This place was my life for over thirty years. I raised you kids here from birth. I lived a lot of life here." She sighed, and her shoulders slumped forward. "I can't believe it's gone."

"It will be very soon." She drew her mother into her arms and fought back another river of tears. "I'm sorry. I tried, Mom."

"I know you did." Her mother smoothed her back. "Thanks for trying."

Fate slid the key into the lock and opened the door. "Let's get this over with. This day's already been the worst. I don't want to end it in a concrete-walled cell. I'm not supposed to have this key."

"Okay." Her mother stepped inside and drew a deep breath, and it was all Fate could do to keep from sitting on the ugly linoleum floor and bawling like a baby.

She'd failed her mother, again. How many times did that make? Hell, she couldn't even begin to count.

"Do you remember when you were little, and you used to roller skate in the living room?"

"Yeah, Mom. I remember."

Her mother walked through the dining room to the kitchen. "And you remember all the fun we had at Christmas? The family room was so full of presents you could hardly walk through it." She chuckled, but Fate knew it was a bittersweet sound, that of a broken-hearted woman who had been beat down by life.

She wondered if someday she'd be doing the same thing, basically living in the past because the present was too painful to endure. She rubbed her mother's shoulders. "Those were great times, Mom. And maybe sometime you'll have those kinds of Christmases with your grandbabies."

"Are you?" Her mother turned and gripped her hands. "Are you trying to tell me something?" Fate was tempted to lie, just to see that hint of hope on her mother's face remain, if only for a little while. But it would be cruel. Unforgivable. Like the kind of lies someone else had told her recently.

She shook her head. "No, I'm afraid not."

"Oh." Her mother dropped her hands and turned away. "Like you said, maybe someday." She meandered through the rest of the main floor, looking uneasy, sad, defeated, much like Fate felt. "They've painted. I hate white walls. Did they have to paint the walls white?"

"I know, Mom. But they like to make it look new. The people who buy the house will use colors, I'm sure."

Her mother nodded then climbed the stairs. "I have to go up."

"Please, just a minute more. I don't want to get caught in here."

"I know. Only a minute." She opened the door at the top of the stairs and stepped into the master bedroom. "They took out my carpet. My beautiful wallpaper. My curtains. They're all gone." She slid to the floor like a wilting flower, awake, yet looking too weak to remain standing. And then she covered her face in her hands. Her shoulders quaked.

Fate watched her mother cry, not having a clue what to do. She'd tried, even endured long hours at that ridiculous tattoo place to keep the house in the family. But this was it. When the bank called her former employer to verify her income, they'd close their doors to her for good. No way in hell she could get another job by the auction. It was only a few days away.

"We'll make a new life together. You can move in with me. It'll be fun."

Her mother dropped her hands, stood and hugged Fate's waist. "Yes. We can do that." She walked out of the room. "I'm ready. Let's go now."

"Okay." More than ready to leave, she followed her mother down the stairs. But no sooner were they at the bottom than her mom was dashing back up them. "Where are you going?"

"I have to check something."

Shaking her head, she followed the distraught woman. What was she doing now?

When she walked around the corner in the master bedroom, she caught her mother stacking boxes on top of one another in the closet. "What are you doing?"

"I want to see if they've cleared out the attic."

"Here, let me. I don't want you to fall." Fate stood on the shaky boxes and pushed up the attic door. She carefully stood on tiptoes. "There are some boxes up here—"

"Thank God! Can you get them?"

"No. I need to get higher."

Her mother gave her rump a shove, a strange feeling being goosed by her own mother. But it worked, and she was able to pull herself into the attic. She handed down four boxes then dropped to the floor and closed the opening. "Can we go now?"

Her mother, hugging one of the boxes to her chest, nodded her head. "Yes, we can go now."

They carried the boxes out to Fate's car, and her mother opened one after the other. The sound of paper crinkled as she sifted through the contents, and her mother sighed. Fate looked over her shoulder.

All four boxes held yellowed paper smudged with faded poster paints, coloring book pictures scribbled with crayons. Lumps of baked clay resembling animals. Her mother blinked back a tear. "How could I go on without these?"

Fate simply nodded and urged her mother into the car. And after one final silent farewell, Fate drove away from her childhood home, down her childhood street, through her childhood subdivision. And away from childhood memories.

After dropping off her despondent mother, she went home, ignored the blinking answering machine and stared at the TV. And once she was so tired she couldn't focus her eyes, she went to bed. The next morning, she felt no better. It was not a good feeling having no place to go on a Tuesday. She glanced at the clock, willing time to move faster, yet it continued to drag by. And as noon approached, she considered canceling her lunch date with John.

Why had she called him anyway? Hell if she could remember anymore...

But, after calling Tracy and enduring a stern lecture on the hazards of becoming a hermit and hiding from life, she pulled her hair back, slipped on a pair of jeans and a t-shirt and headed for the restaurant.

Despite her best efforts to dillydally, she got there first. So she sat, alone, and watched neighboring diners chatter.

"I thought I might find you here."

No way! That lying, scheming, asshole hadn't hunted her down. She didn't look, couldn't stomach the thought of looking at him. "If that's you, Gabe, you'd better leave now before I punch your lights out. I'm on a date."

He stepped into her line of sight, and her stomach twisted into a tight ball. "Yeah? Funny, I don't see anyone sitting next to you."

Damn him! The cocky, annoying, obnoxious Gabe was back. In full force. In the flesh. In her face. "Get lost."

"I tried to call you. Did you get my message?"

"No. I didn't bother listening to it. I don't want to hear any more of your lies."

"I wasn't lying. Won't you just give me a chance to explain?"

"Why? So you can get laid? Why don't you flash that tongue around the restaurant, and I'd bet you'd get at least a few takers." Someone cleared their throat, and she glanced over her shoulder to see who it was. John. "Hi. Thanks for coming." She stood, purposely ignoring Gabe, and took John's hand. She motioned toward Gabe. "Just ignore him. He's leaving."

Gabe stuck his hand out. "Gabe Ryan. I work with Fate."

"Correction, worked. I don't work there anymore," Fate said.

John glanced at both of them then gave Gabe's hand a shake. "Good to meet you. I'm John. And we're on a date, if you don't mind."

Gabe pulled up a chair from the next table and took a seat—the nerve he had! "Actually, I do care."

"Gabe, I swear, I'll kill you." She shoved his shoulder. "Get the hell out of here. No one invited you. Why are you doing this to me?"

"Because you haven't given me the chance to explain. Give me that much and I'll leave you alone for good."

That was tempting, if he'd keep his word. But the problem was she knew if he told her something that even remotely made sense, she'd buy it. And the last thing she wanted to do was fall for another one of his lies. She was simply too vulnerable. "Not now."

Gabe leaned forward, and her nerve endings caught fire. "When?"

"Later. Call me later."

"Fair enough." He stood, gave John an obvious once-over—rude son of a bitch—and nodded his head. "I'll call you later. Nice meeting you, John. Don't touch her. She's mine."

She jumped to her feet. "In your dreams, you sick son—"

John caught her wrist and silently pleaded for her to stop. She sat.

"Want to tell me what that's all about?" he asked.

"It's a long story."

"That's okay." He flagged the waitress. "Tuesdays are slow. I have at least a couple of hours."

To his credit, John was a good listener. He spent the next two hours bobbing his head up and down as she poured out all the ugly details from the past couple of weeks. Then he wished her luck, shook her hand, and left.

She wouldn't be seeing him anytime soon.

With nowhere else to go, she headed home and busied herself cleaning closets, figuring she'd give herself the rest of the week to clear her head before hitting the pavement and looking for another job. A full week off would be nice, give her a chance to do things she normally didn't have the time to do, like go to museums, do grocery shopping without the weekend crowds, think.

Her phone rang, and expecting it was either Tracy or Gabe, she read the caller ID display.

Work. Probably Gabe.

The machine beeped and clicked and she waited for his voice.

"Hello, this is Curtis Duncan. I'm calling for Fate Doherty. If she would—"

She picked up the phone to take the call. "Hello?"

"Ms. Doherty?"

"Yes."

"I'm calling because I need to meet with you. Can you come to the office?"

"No offense, but if this is just a formality to my being fired, I can live without it."

"Not at all. You're still very much an employee here. Whatever gave you that idea?"

"What? But...wait a minute. Did Gabe put you up to something?"

"I have no idea what you mean. How does three o'clock sound?"

She glanced up at the clock. "I can do that."

"Good. See you then. Goodbye, Ms. Doherty."

She changed her clothes and retamed her hair with the help of her trusty scrunchy then drove to Single Temptation—she'd never get used to that name. She stepped up to his door at exactly three o'clock.

"Ms. Doherty." He motioned her inside, and she took a seat.

Curiosity was eating her alive, but she didn't speak.

"A lot of crazy things have been happening around here lately, and I felt, after Monday morning's confusion, that I should get the explanations taken care of before any assumptions were made."

She shifted in her chair. "I think it's a little too late for that."

He nodded. "I should have talked to you sooner, but you left so abruptly, and I haven't been able to reach you."

"You've been trying?"

He nodded. "Anyway, that's not the issue I called you in here to discuss."

She silently prepared herself for a surprise, figured it had to be something she'd least expect for him to have called her in like he had.

"Mr. Ryan has left the company."

The words kind of soaked into her consciousness. "What? Left?" That made no sense! Why would he lie to her, scheme, backstab and then leave? "I thought—"

"Like I said, I figured we'd best clear the air before any assumptions were made."

"But what about the meeting? Why wasn't I a part of it?"

"Mr. Ryan was covering for you. He thought you were going to be out for the day."

Had she been that foolish? Been willing—hell, more than willing—to believe the worst when all along she'd been wrong? Gabe had wanted to explain, but she hadn't given him the chance... "Covering for me?"

"That's what a good assistant does for their boss, isn't it, Ms. Doherty?"

"Assistant?" What? She was confused.

"He took a demotion over a week ago."

Those words landed on her head like a load of concrete. He took a demotion. He left the company. He had covered for her.

And she'd called him every ugly name in the book. All because she assumed—God, she hated that word!—he was lying to her. He hadn't wanted her job. Could she be any stupider? Any meaner? After everything he'd done to help her. She had to make it right. She couldn't live with herself until she did. "Do you know where he's gone?"

"No."

"Why did he quit?"

"For legal reasons I can't tell you that. Maybe you should find him and ask him yourself." He lifted a manila folder from his desktop. "Now, I reviewed your personnel file this morning, and I see you have some vacation time carried over from last year. I'd like to see you take that now, before the new company gets fully underway. Would you like to take the next week off?"

Her head was swimming. What had he said? "Sure."

"Okay. Then we'll see you bright and early next Monday morning." He stood.

She stood, too. "Okay. Monday."

This wasn't happening. She'd made such a fool out of herself, all because she hadn't—even after sleeping with Gabe , even after hours of talking, sharing, laughing—been able to believe anything but the worst about him.

She didn't deserve his love or forgiveness.

After all, what had she done for him? Absolutely nothing.

She reached for the doorknob and gripped it in her hand. "Oh God."

"What is it, Ms. Doherty?" Duncan asked from behind her.

"Nothing. Sorry. Just thinking. I'll see you Monday. Thanks for clearing things up for me."

"See you Monday."

She left the building, ran to her car, and started it up. Now, where to? Where would she find him? She had to find him. Had to talk to him. Had to apologize. Had to make this right.

He didn't deserve the trash she'd hurled at him.

Fighting to remember how to find his place, she drove across town. It took her over two hours but she was successful. Too bad he wasn't there.

She tried his cell phone. Off. She left a message on his answering machine. She left a note on his door. She checked with the neighbor.

The elderly gentleman said he'd seen Gabe moving boxes out of his apartment yesterday.

He'd moved? He'd left? But he'd wanted to explain. He said he would call. Had she hurt him that bad?

Oh no.

She drove home, her heart so low she'd need a spatula to scrape it off the floor. Her belly ached. Her head hurt. Her insides were knotted.

He had to call.

The phone rang, and she jumped to answer it. "Hello?"

"Hey, Fate!" Tracy said. "What's up? How was the date with John?"

"Well, if you think me rehashing my love affair with another man a great date, then my date with John was a huge success."

"That bad?"

Fate slumped into a nearby chair. "It's worse than that. I'm an idiot."

"You are not."

"I was all wrong about Gabe. I just wanted to believe the worst about him. I couldn't give him the benefit of the doubt. And now he's gone. I don't know where to find him. I want to at least apologize."

"That man can't stay away from you for long. I'm sure you'll get your chance."

"But apologizing isn't good enough. I haven't done anything to deserve what he's given me. He's done so much."

"Well, what does he want more than anything?"

Fate closed her eyes and thought about that question for a moment, tried to remember their conversations. "Just me, I guess. My trust? The one thing I kept denying him — and a belly ring." She chuckled remembering that conversation.

"Well, then do it. Get your bellybutton pierced. And when he does get in touch with you, do something to prove you believe in him."

"Okay." Her stomach flip-flopped. "Will you go with me?"

"Sure. I'm getting off work in a few. I'll come over and pick you up."

"Okay." She changed into a scrubby pair of sweats with a low waistband and a t-shirt and waited for Tracy. And as they drove to *Original Skin*, they chatted about the crazy things people did for love and how much it lowered your IQ.

And when she entered the building, Paul gave her a big smile. "See? I told you you wouldn't be able to stay away." He gave Tracy an appraising once over and an even bigger smile. "Who's your friend?"

"This is my best friend, Tracy. Tracy, Paul."

They shook hands, and Fate couldn't miss the sparks flying between them. Funny, she'd never in a million years expect those two to be attracted to each other, Tracy so conservative and Paul so...unconventional. She teared up, the mysteries of love.

Paul led them back to a private room. "So, who's the patient today? Tracy?"

"No. Not today. Fate's getting her bellybutton pierced."

Paul raised his eyebrows. "Really? After this past weekend, that's the last thing I expected." He motioned toward the chair, which mildly resembled a torture device, or an electric chair, and Fate sat, her stomach in her throat. "Are you nervous?"

"Yes." That was an understatement!

"It'll only hurt for a split second. And then you'll be sore for a few days. Clean it twice daily with soap and water and put a dab of petroleum jelly on the jewelry and work it through the piercing after you wash." He handed her a card with care instructions. "You can read this at home when you can concentrate better." Then he prepared his instruments, and Fate refused to watch. "Did you pick out your jewelry yet?"

"Oh! I forgot."

"I'll do it." Tracy jumped up and left the room.

Paul watched her leave. "She's cute. Is she taken?"

"Not at all. You should ask her out. I think she likes you."

He grinned. "Just for that, the piercing's on the house." He pinched her stomach and zap! Pain shot up her spine as the blade went in. Her skin was tugged and pulled and then everything was still, and she realized her eyelids were clamped shut. "You can open them now."

"Are we done yet?"

"Just waiting for the jewelry."

She nodded but didn't look.

Tracy returned a moment later and handed Paul a plastic packet. He opened it and started tugging on Fate's skin again.

"Are you doing okay?" Tracy asked.

"Yeah." She swallowed, sure something was on its way up from her stomach.

"All done," Paul said. "Take a look."

Fate forced her eyes open and snuck a quick peek. There, in the middle of her belly button hung a deep blue stone. And up above was a sparkling clear one. "Oh."

"Okay. Do what I said. You don't want it to get infected, and I'll see you Saturday, right?"

"Sure." She stood, and black and white stars glittered before her eyes, blocking out her vision. "Oh. I know I'm a coward, but I don't want to faint. Gabe'll hear about it. Get me out of here."

"Okay." Tracy took her hand and led her outside.

Breathless and just about blind, Fate sat on the grass and ducked her head between her knees. "What I do for love."

"What we all do. Welcome to the club, Fate."

Chapter Thirteen
*Happiness is possible, even for someone
who has been shunned by fate.*

"It's done," Duncan said. "She was shocked as hell. It was all over her face."

"Thanks. Sorry it came to this. I thought we might be able to work things out different, but I guess that's not going to happen."

"Yeah, yeah. You knew it would end like this all along. I still think you're an idiot, but what the hell do I know. Just don't repay me by working for my competition."

"Promise."

"Later, Ryan. Good luck with her."

"Thanks." Gabe punched the talk button on his cell. Where would she be now? Had she gone to find him? Had she gone home? His cell phone rang again. "Hello?"

"Heya, Ryan. It's Paul."

"What's up?"

"Just thought I'd let you know your girlfriend was just in here. I won't spoil the surprise, but if I were you, I'd hightail it over to her place. You're in for a big surprise. And I'm jealous as hell."

What had she done? "What kind of surprise?" He felt a goofy grin spread over his face. She'd done something for him?

She did love him! His heart soared. He slammed his car into gear and roared down the street, knowing if it took him two minutes to get there it would be too long.

"I'm not saying another word. Bye." Paul hung up.

Ungrateful bastard!

It took twelve minutes and thirteen seconds—he'd counted every one of them—to get to her place. He almost continued driving when he saw a car in the driveway. Did it belong to that guy, John? Had Paul made an assumption?

Well, he was here now! He'd taken enough risks already, what was one more? He parked and forced himself to walk up to the door. It opened before he had the chance to knock.

A young woman stood on the other side, a curious expression on her face. "May I help you?"

"I'm here to see Fate. I'm Gabe."

"Oh!" Her gaze swept up and down then she stepped aside. "The one-and-only Gabe. I've heard all about you."

"All good, I hope." He chuckled, knowing full well she'd probably heard everything but good.

"Of course." She closed the door behind him. "Fate's lying down." She reached behind him and picked up a brown leather purse. "And I was just leaving."

"Is she sick?"

"No, she's fine. Just a bit of a baby. I'm sure you can handle her." She opened the door. "Nice meeting you, Gabe." And then she left.

A bit of a baby? Fate? Never! If she was in bed this early, not even eight o'clock in the evening, something must be really wrong. He hurried back to her bedroom, memories from not so long ago shooting through his mind and giving him one hell of a hard-on.

He knocked and opened the bedroom door. The room was dark. Was she sleeping? He went up to the bed. "Fate?"

"Gabe?" She sat up and reached for the lamp on the bedside table. The light snapped on, emitting a mellow light over her face and sweatshirt. She smiled.

Damn, that was one dazzling smile! He rushed to her side and swept her into his arms, but she instantly stiffened. He pulled back. "What's wrong?"

"It's nothing. I just…" She hooked the band of her sweatshirt in her fingertips and raised it. Something flashed in the dim light.

"What did you do?"

"I got my bellybutton pierced. For you."

He sat on the bed and leaned down to get a closer look. "You crazy woman! I can't believe you did that." He kissed the red flesh around the jewelry, feeling her muscles tense under his lips.

"I had to do something. It's not much, I know. But I've been so stupid. I can't believe I thought you were lying to me, after everything—"

He raised his index finger to her lips. "Shush. I understand. You don't need to rehash it all. All that matters is we're here, together. That's all I've ever wanted."

"You did say so, once or twice." She leaned forward, palmed his cheeks and smiled into his eyes. "And that you can have. For as long as you like."

"Forever?"

"Are you sure you can deal with me for that long? I'm such a pain in the ass sometimes."

He returned her smile. "A good pain in the ass. My pain in the ass. I don't want to live another day without you. I've known that since the first day we met in college."

She shook her head and dropped her hands. "If only I hadn't been so blind. I've made you wait so long."

"It was worth every minute if you're mine now."

"Absolutely."

"So, will you trust me?"

"Yes."

"No second guessing me?"

"Nope."

"Okay." He stood. "Are you ready for the adventure of a lifetime?"

She grinned.

Oh yeah, he liked the hint of devil in that expression! "I take it that means yes?"

"You bet."

"Then are you in for a surprise!" Fate watched as he clapped his hands together then rubbed them, his expression wicked and gleeful all at once. Oh, boy! She'd seen that look. And then ended up bound and fucked until she couldn't see straight.

And it had been heaven.

Hot juices instantly slicked her pussy. What would it be this time? She couldn't even imagine.

"Where's my bag?"

"Under the bed." She hadn't moved it since the last time they'd made love. Hadn't peeked inside, either. She'd learned to appreciate Gabe Ryan surprises.

He stooped down, and she listened to him grumble and groan as he shimmied under the bed to get it. Then she heard the zipper, the clank of metal, and duller sounds of plastic. "Perfect." He stood, something held behind his back. "You trust me completely, don't you?"

She didn't hesitate. "Yes, I trust you with my life. My body. My future."

"Good." He grinned and pulled an arm out from behind his back. "Let's make a movie."

"A movie of what?" She watched him uncover the lens and peer into the scope. He wanted to film her? "Oh, no." *Well, maybe.* She tingled from head to toe. And an all-too-familiar heat settled between her legs. She wiggled out from under the covers and watched those sexy lips of his lift in an appreciative smile. "For you, anything."

He nodded. "That's wonderful, baby. I'm so grateful. This will be something to remember for when we're old and gray. You'll see."

"But I need music." She stood and flipped on her radio, hitting the button for the CD player. Mellow jazz filled the room.

Perfect. Still, she felt a little weird, uncomfortable. "What do you want me to do?"

"Strip for me. Show me how much you want me."

She closed her eyes and tried to imagine herself somewhere else. In one of those bars, stripping for an audience of one. One sexy, irresistible man. She swayed to the music.

"That's it, baby. Take off your clothes. Dance for me."

She started with her sweatshirt, taking her time lifting the hem up higher and higher until her lacy bra was exposed. Then she made quick work of disposing it. Next, she unhooked her bra, encouraged by Gabe's periodic whoops and growls. She slid the straps off her shoulders, holding the lace cups up over her breasts with her hands. Then she pushed one cup aside, exposing her nipple.

She teased it with her fingers, circling and pinching until it was an achy pebble and then did the same with the other.

Bra forgotten, she moved on to her sweatpants. She shimmied as she slid them over her hips, turning around so when she bent over, he had a full view of her behind. She exaggerated her bending, knees straight, ass exposed.

He groaned, and her pussy throbbed. "You're driving me crazy. You know just what to do, what I like. And I can't wait to do the same for you."

"You already are." She reached between her legs, feeling the hot juices saturating her cotton thong.

"I want to see everything. Show me."

Still bent over, she spread her cheeks and pulled her thong aside.

"Oh, yeah. Touch yourself. Your ass."

His requests were sending throbbing heat to her pussy, making her crazy with need. The minute he was inside, she'd come. No doubt about it.

"Wait a minute." She heard him step away for a split second, then return. "Okay. Take this and go to the bed. I want to watch." He handed her the vibrator and a tube of KY.

She took the goodies to the bed. "Where to?"

"Hands and knees on the bed. Ass toward me. You know how I love your ass. Tell me how much you want to please me."

"I am going to make you so hot for me you'll beg for mercy." She discarded the thong, feeling the most amazing sense of exposure and anticipation. Her pussy was so hot and wet and needy she could cry. She gathered several pillows and rested her chest on them, then reached around to spread her cheeks.

"Oh, yeah. That's it. You like showing your ass to me, don't you? It makes you hot."

"Yes. My God, yes."

"Now, the vibrator. On your ass."

She turned it on, smoothed on some KY over her anus and explored herself with the buzzing tip. It sent humming energy through her whole body. Her muscles tensed, right down to her toes.

"How does it feel, baby?"

"Oh!"

"Inside. Fuck your ass."

She concentrated on relaxing her asshole, willing it to open. But it was impossible. So turned on her pussy was nearly in spasm, she couldn't possibly relax a muscle south of her waist. She pushed the vibrator inside, and the buzz shot through her body, shoving her over the edge and into an explosive, convulsing orgasm.

"Oh, yeah, baby. Come for me. That's it. Show the camera all those sweet juices. Part your cheeks."

It was so hard for her to think in the midst of an orgasm, her body wracked by tremors. But she did what he said, feeling him close, filming her ass clenching and unclenching around the vibrator.

When the orgasm eased to a twitch, she pulled it out and glanced over her shoulder. The camera was inches from her pussy. And Gabe had the most amazing expression on his face.

He looked like he'd fuck her all night long. That was one expression she couldn't ignore.

Oh, yes. She was ready. Thrilled, she rolled over onto her back and spread her thighs as wide as she could. "Do you like what you see? Want to see more?"

"Hell, yes! Show me more."

She chuckled at his obvious eagerness, wishing he'd ditch the camera and make love to her. She was hot for him, her pussy demanded him inside. Her body begged for his embrace. But, judging from his wide eyes and huge smile, he hadn't lost control yet and wouldn't give up recording. She would have to make him lose control.

How?

She began slowly, parting her labia and making circles over her clit. It was still supersensitive after that last orgasm, and she had to use a light touch. But slowly, the biting edge evaporated, leaving the familiar pleasant feeling of growing arousal. She lifted her other hand to her breast and played with her nipples. *Dammit, what did they usually say in those movies?* "See how hot I am for you? My pussy wants you so bad." *Oh Lord, please don't let me laugh.*

He growled but didn't move from his position, hovering over her, camera in front of his face.

Knowing she was being filmed was driving her crazy. Heat spread out across her body, and her thigh muscles tightened. "I need you. Inside."

"Just a little bit more."

Her eyes were clamped closed, and she couldn't force them open. A million images flashed through her mind as she teased her clit and breasts mercilessly for him, for the camera.

Something tickled her stomach, stroking up and down. Smooth. She glanced down.

A dildo. One huge dildo.

She gripped it in her hand. It felt almost like the real thing—nah. On went some KY, and then she teased her pussy with the tip. Damn, that felt good!

"This is great, love. You're so willing to please me. So eager to try things, to explore with me. We'll have a lifetime to discover each other."

She slipped it inside. "Oh!" It wasn't Gabe, but it was damn near close.

"Oh, yeah. Imagine it's me loving you. Fill your sweet pussy with it."

Okay. She could do that. And it might just send her over the brink again. She was so close every muscle in her body was tense. Her breath came in and out in a fast rasp. Her heart thumped in her ears.

She pushed that dildo into her pussy, slid it in oh so slowly, enjoying every inch. "Oh, God!"

"Don't come yet."

What? Like she could stop that? She fought the surging waves of throbbing heat and remained perfectly still.

"That's it. Don't come. Wait."

Easy for you to say, lover! She opened her eyes and watched him film her pussy gripping that huge sex toy.

Seeing it almost sent her over the edge. She clamped her eyelids closed again.

"Absolutely gorgeous. Look at all those sweet juices. I can't wait to bury my cock inside you."

Do it!

"And those breasts. So perfect. I can't wait to bite and suckle them."

"For God's sake, do it! You're killing me, here."

"Just keep holding on. Take out the dildo."

She slid it out, and sagged with relief as her empty pussy relaxed.

"Now, put it back in."

"What?" She looked at him, another blade of need shot through her body. "I hate this. You're teasing me. I'm going crazy."

"Trust me. I'm going to make it wonderful, just like you have for me."

She nodded, dropped her head back to the bed and slowly slid it back inside, trying like hell not to succumb to the spasms threatening to shake her whole body. Her pussy gripped it, sending a rush of heat up her body. Oh, shit!

"Don't come. You hear me?"

"I can't stop it."

"Stop it, now!"

She yanked the dildo out, just before the first spasm, and threw it at him. "You jerk! Get over here and fuck me."

He laughed. "Now, we watch."

"Watch what?"

"Your movie." He walked to the TV and fiddled with the wires. Within seconds, she was sitting on the edge of the bed watching herself stripping. It was a weird feeling, seeing all the bumps and imperfections glaring at her on film. Her fanny was too big, her breasts too small. And there was—oh no!—cellulite on her thighs.

"How can you get turned on by this? I look terrible!"

He glanced down at his groin. "I'm so hard right now, I could drill through diamonds. You're the most gorgeous woman I've ever seen. Look at those curves, those tits. You *are* all woman. My woman. Your body drives me crazy. It always will."

She tried to see herself through his eyes, tried to appreciate the softness, the smooth skin and curves. Her pussy started to tingle as she watched herself part her buttocks for him. The camera zoomed in to her tight little hole as she teased it with the vibrator. Memories of how that felt left her pussy weeping.

"Look at you, submitting, trusting me. That drives me absolutely insane."

She watched, heat spreading up to her scalp. Having him take command truly turned her on. She loved submitting to him. She loved pleasing him.

She loved him.

She needed him. Inside. Her pussy was screaming to be filled. She stood, pushed his shoulders down until he was lying on the bed, a smile on lips she was sure would taste sweet.

And as she bent down to sample them, she slid a hand down to his shirt hem and lifted, exposing his tight stomach. "These clothes have to go." He shifted his weight, allowing her to strip him from the waist up. Then he watched as she unbuttoned his pants and discarded those, too. Left only in a pair of very snug, very sexy black athletic boxers that hugged his erection and balls, he looked like a model in a magazine ad.

Her core twitched and she felt herself heating under his gray-eyed gaze. He watched her, his gaze blatantly resting alternately on her pussy and breasts as she moved.

She slid his boxers off—not the easiest thing to do, thanks to his huge erection—a drop on its tip. It twitched as she stroked, and her pussy dripped along with it. "I want you."

"Show me. Show me how much you want me. How much you need me. You can see how much I want you."

She teased the head and underside of his penis with her tongue and teeth.

"Oh, baby! You're so sweet, so giving."

She stroked his testicles, sucked on them, fingered his ass. He parted his legs, giving her free access to this tight hole as her head bobbed up and down, his erection sliding up and down her throat.

She laid back against the headboard and parted her legs. "I'm so wet for you."

"It turns me on to know how much you want me. That you're mine." My God, that look was so hot she thought she'd burst into flames.

She spread wider and slid her finger inside, feeling the smooth muscles tighten around it. Hot, slick juices coated her finger as she plunged it in and out. Then she lifted her hand to his face. "Do you want a taste?"

He licked the finger clean. "Like honey. More."

She skirted around, teasing and tugging her labia, drawing small, slow circles over her clit until the muscles of her ass and stomach clenched. Then she plunged her finger inside again. "See how tight I am? Tight and hot only for you."

He dropped his face, burying it between her legs and coaxing her hand away. His tongue took over, circling her clit, delving inside her pussy, laving her folds, exploring her ass. Her feet curled, her breathing all but ceased. He glanced up and smiled at her, his face wet from her juices. "Are you ready to be loved?"

She nodded, unable to speak.

He spread her legs wider, holding her knees with his hands, and pushed deep inside.

"Oh!" That instant feeling of fullness just about sent her over the edge.

"Don't come. Not yet."

She wanted so badly to comply. To show him how much she adored him. She forced herself to relax around him, an almost impossible task.

"That's it. Save it for me. Enjoy the feelings. We are one. Our bodies. Our souls. Our minds."

She closed her eyes and enjoyed the smells of her juices, sweet and musty in the air. She concentrated on the taste of him on her lips, licking them and savoring the flavor lingering there.

Then, she rejoiced on the sounds of his low groans and quickened breathing. He inhaled deeply, his pelvis slapping loudly against her ass as he drove into her over and over again. It was such a sexy sound. Skin against skin. That unique sound made only during fucking.

"That's it, baby. You are so good. So good." He ground into her, his cock touching every part of her deep inside. It hit her cervix, sending pleasure and pain shooting up her spine. She stiffened then relaxed as it moved away.

"Touch yourself."

There was no way she could do that and not come. Not when his huge cock was inside, her pussy tight around him. She slowly slid her hand down, her palm resting on her mound.

"That's it, honey. Touch yourself."

She made small circles over her clit, relishing the luxurious warmth that spread out as each circle was completed. Oh, that was amazing. Him inside, her clit throbbing. She felt the telling heat of an impending climax zip through her body and pinched her clit.

Her pussy throbbed then relaxed.

"Rub that little button for me."

"I'm so close."

"Do it." He didn't speak those words, he growled them.

And thank God! She'd come all over that huge cock of his. She obeyed, allowing the circles to quicken, meeting his pace as he pumped into her. In a heartbeat, she was soaring on heated waves. Her body shook in spasms as electricity shot through every cell. Never had she had an orgasm like that. She thought she might just quit breathing and die.

"Oh, yeah!" He growled loudly and then fucked her like a madman.

She felt wetness seeping from her pussy as he drove his seed deep inside. And then, spent, her body twitching, her legs weak, she stilled and enjoyed the weight of his limp body on hers. "Gabe?"

"Yeah," he said between gasping breaths. He rolled to his side and propped his head in his hand.

"I love you." A flood of emotion pounded through her body as if those three words had liberated her. She cried. Tears of joy, of relief, of guilt.

He smiled and gathered her into his arms. "I love you, too. More than I could ever say. I'll spend the rest of my life showing you."

"You already have. I'm sorry for doubting you—"

He pressed his forefinger to her lips. "No more, Fate. We already talked about it. I'm happy. You're happy... You *are* happy aren't you?"

She nodded.

He thumbed a tear hanging from her jaw. "We're together. That's all that matters."

"But what about your job?"

"Well, I just might have to take a position with Dates-R-Us—"

"No way! We're not working for competitors again! We're a team. End of story."

"Fair enough. I could use a change. And speaking of change, where's your suitcase?"

"What?" The man wasn't going anywhere now, was he?

He laughed. "Where's your suitcase?"

"Under the bed."

He rose up on hands and knees, his cock still deep inside. "Then let's pack. And pack for warm weather. By the way, does your mother have any problems with water?"

"None that I know of." What was he talking about?

"Good, she can go with us." He slid out of her—a terrible thing—got off the bed, and bent over, gathering his clothes.

"But, wait. If we're going somewhere, I need to take care of the house—"

"Done."

"But how?"

"I'll explain later." Once dressed, he swept her into his arms and dropped her on her feet. "Now, let's get going. We have a flight to catch." He bent down, retrieved the suitcase and dropped it on the bed. "I'll be right back. I need to make a few phone calls."

"Okay." Completely bewildered, still light-headed from that mind-blowing orgasm, and weak in the knees, she watched him leave the room.

What was he up to now? Fate had the feeling this surprise would be the best ever.

Epilogue

Fate stared into Gabe's eyes, hoping she'd remember this day forever. The smell of the salty ocean air, the heat of the sun, the cool breeze. The look of love on Gabe's handsome face.

"And I, Fate Doherty, take this man to be my husband. For richer, for poorer, in sickness and in health, until death do us part."

She slid the gold band on his finger then looked up into his face. They both, at the same time, looked at each other and smiled. He was so happy. She'd made him happy.

He deserved that, and so much more.

Moments later, they kissed and were accepting congratulations from the other cruise passengers and from Fate's mother. She hadn't looked so glowing in years. The sun, the fresh air, it had done wonders for the woman. And she loved him so much more for this gift.

They spent a couple of hours, maybe less, dancing on the deck to the mellow soul music performed by a small band. And then, Gabe tugged her toward the stairs.

It was time.

She smiled inwardly. Since they left Detroit, two days ago, Gabe had refused to touch her. That had been hell, and she hadn't understood why until today. She was quite certain he wanted this first time, as man and wife to be special. He'd make up for it tonight.

No sooner did they step into their room, than Gabe had his mouth on her neck. She tipped her head back, relishing the goose bumps erupting on her arms and legs, and slid her hands down to the bulge in his pants. She rubbed up and down, wishing he'd get rid of the tux.

His fingers fiddled with the back of her dress. "Damn if this isn't the most impossible dress!"

She giggled, having forgotten that the dress she'd chosen from the ship's large stock had a row of tiny buttons running from mid-back to the small of her back. "Do you need some help?"

"Nope. Are you kidding me? The struggle is half the fun." He flipped on the light. "That's better. I like to see…everything." The dress was off in seconds.

Then her bra, panties and stockings. He removed her garter with his teeth.

"Now, this isn't fair. Off with your clothes. I like to see everything, too." She slid her hands in his jacket and pushed it off his shoulders, then worked each button on his shirt. He helped her by getting rid of his shoes, socks, pants and shorts.

Finally! That gorgeous body was hers for the taking. She pushed his chest, until he was leaning back against the bed. "You made me wait for two long days—"

"Well, I'm yours now. Take me." He dropped flat on the bed, his arms spread wide. "Do what you will. Be tender."

She crawled on hands and knees over him and began at his neck, kissing, sucking, nipping his skin. He smelled good and tasted even better. A rush of heat settled between her legs and her arms trembled.

She moved lower, over a wide chest and flat stomach and followed the line of hair to his thick cock, erect and ready for her. It would be so easy to slide right down the length, take him inside. But not yet. She wanted this time to be special, different.

Instead, she took him in her mouth, opening wide to take him down deep in her throat. He groaned, and her pussy throbbed. Damn, she wanted him. She slid up, flicked her tongue over the pink head, followed the ridge around it and gripped the base in her hand. When she slid her hand up and down, in unison with her mouth, his hips started rocking.

And then, rolling onto his side, he pulled her off. "You keep doing that and I'll come."

"Would that be such a bad thing?"

"Yes. I want my seed in you. I want to have a baby with you."

Those words sent a rush of tears to her eyes. "A baby?"

"You meant it when you said you want to have kids, didn't you?"

"Oh, yes!"

"Good!" In a stealth move she hadn't seen coming, he flipped her on her back, opened her legs wide and teased her clit with that wonderful pierced tongue of his. Waves of throbbing heat shot from her pussy out, warming her from head to toe. She could feel herself getting closer, nearing that crest.

And just as the first pulse of her orgasm shot through her body, he plunged inside. He pulled out slowly then slid in, burying himself deep. Her muscles clenched and unclenched around him, and as she opened her eyes, she saw him tense as he found his own release. His movements quickened as he thrust inside, planting his seed deep in her womb. She found a second crest as he drilled into her in a frenzy, screaming out the only words that could reach her lips, "I love you."

And as their bodies relaxed, her heartbeat returning to a normal pace and her breathing slowing, he held her tight.

"I love you, too, my wife. Fate brought us together that first day in college. And fate brought us together again now. I will *never* take fate for granted again." He kissed the top of her head. "And I will never stop loving you."

"So, tell me." She stroked his chest, her insides burning for more of him. "How did you take care of the house?"

"I told them I was your husband."

She laughed. "Seems you gave fate a little shove."

He smiled. "Well, I couldn't leave it all to her whim. After all, half the fun in life is tempting fate."

About the author:

Nothing exciting happens in Tawny Taylor's life, unless you count giving the cat a flea dip--a cat can make some fascinating sounds when immersed chin-deep in insecticide--or chasing after a houseful of upchucking kids during flu season. She doesn't travel the world or employ a staff of personal servants. She's not even built like a runway model. She's just your run-of-the-mill, pleasantly plump Detroit suburban mom and wife. That's why she writes, for the sheer joy of it. She doesn't need to escape, mind you. Despite being run-of-the-mill, her life is wonderful. She just likes to add some...zip. Her heroines might resemble herself, or her next door neighbor (sorry Sue), but they are sure to be memorable (she hopes!). And her heroes--inspired by movie stars, her favorite television actors or her husband--are fully capable of delivering one hot happily-ever-after after another. Combined, the characters and plots she weaves bring countless hours of enjoyment to Tawny...and she hopes to readers too! In the end, that's all the matters to Tawny, bringing a little bit of zip to someone else's life.

Tawny welcomes mail from readers. You can write to her c/o Ellora's Cave Publishing at 1056 Home Avenue, Akron OH 44310-3502.

Why an electronic book?

We live in the Information Age — an exciting time in the history of human civilization in which technology rules supreme and continues to progress in leaps and bounds every minute of every hour of every day. For a multitude of reasons, more and more avid literary fans are opting to purchase e-books instead of paperbacks. The question to those not yet initiated to the world of electronic reading is simply: *why?*

1. *Price.* An electronic title at Ellora's Cave Publishing runs anywhere from 40-75% less than the cover price of the <u>exact same title</u> in paperback format. Why? Cold mathematics. It is less expensive to publish an e-book than it is to publish a paperback, so the savings are passed along to the consumer.

2. *Space.* Running out of room to house your paperback books? That is one worry you will never have with electronic novels. For a low one-time cost, you can purchase a handheld computer designed specifically for e-reading purposes. Many e-readers are larger than the average handheld, giving you plenty of screen room. Better yet, hundreds of titles can be stored within your new library — a single microchip. (Please note that Ellora's Cave does not endorse any specific brands. You can check our website at www.ellorascave.com for customer recommendations we make available to new consumers.)

3. *Mobility.* Because your new library now consists of only a microchip, your entire cache of books can be taken with you wherever you go.

4. *Personal preferences are accounted for.* Are the words you are currently reading too small? Too large? Too...ANNOYING? Paperback books cannot be modified according to personal preferences, but e-books can.

5. *Innovation.* The way you read a book is not the only advancement the Information Age has gifted the literary community with. There is also the factor of what you can read. Ellora's Cave Publishing will be introducing a new line of interactive titles that are available in e-book format only.

6. *Instant gratification.* Is it the middle of the night and all the bookstores are closed? Are you tired of waiting days—sometimes weeks—for online and offline bookstores to ship the novels you bought? Ellora's Cave Publishing sells instantaneous downloads 24 hours a day, 7 days a week, 365 days a year. Our e-book delivery system is 100% automated, meaning your order is filled as soon as you pay for it.

Those are a few of the top reasons why electronic novels are displacing paperbacks for many an avid reader. As always, Ellora's Cave Publishing welcomes your questions and comments. We invite you to email us at service@ellorascave.com or write to us directly at: 1056 Home Avenue, Akron OH 44310-3502.

NEED A MORE EXCITING
WAY TO PLAN YOUR DAY?

ELLORA'S
CAVEMEN
2006 CALENDAR

COMING THIS FALL

THE ELLORA'S CAVE LIBRARY

Stay up to date with Ellora's Cave Titles in Print with our Quarterly Catalog.

TO RECIEVE A CATALOG,
SEND AN EMAIL WITH YOUR NAME
AND MAILING ADDRESS TO:

CATALOG@ELLORASCAVE.COM

OR SEND A LETTER OR POSTCARD
WITH YOUR MAILING ADDRESS TO:
CATALOG REQUEST
c/o ELLORA'S CAVE PUBLISHING, INC.
1337 COMMERCE DRIVE #13
STOW, OH 44224

Lady Jaided

The premier magazine for today's sensual woman

Lady Jaided magazine is devoted to exploring the sexuality and sensuality of women. While there are many similarities between the sexual experiences of men and women, there are just as many if not more differences. Our focus is on the female experience and on giving voice and credence to it. Lady Jaided will include everything from trends, politics, science and history to gossip, humor and celebrity interviews, but our focus will remain on female sexuality and sensuality.

A Sneak Peek at Upcoming Stories

Clan of the Cave Woman
Women's sexuality throughout history.

The Sarandon Syndrome
What's behind the attraction between older women and younger men.

The Last Taboo
Why some women – even feminists – have bondage fantasies

Girls' Eyes for Queer Guys
An in-depth look at the attraction between straight women and gay men

Available Spring 2005

www.LadyJaided.com

Discover for yourself why readers can't get enough of the multiple award-winning publisher Ellora's Cave. Whether you prefer e-books or paperbacks, be sure to visit EC on the web at www.ellorascave.com for an erotic reading experience that will leave you breathless.

www.ellorascave.com

Printed in the United States
30777LVS00003B/67-438

9 781419 950636